IN THE TREE'S SHADOW

A collection of stories that exist in your dreams... and nightmares.

D. L. Finn

Contents

IN THE TREE'S SHADOW v

Also By D. L. Finn vii

Acknowledgments ix

End Of The Road 1

Old Gray Cat 13

The Playdate 14

It's Only A Dream 18

A Reminder 35

A Man On The Pier 36

In The Shadows 39

The Dolphin 46

Lyrical Dragon 50

This Journey 61

The Bench 62

When The Lights Go Out 65

In That Moment 75

The Boy 82

Deadline 86

The Last Ride Of The Night 97

Faith 100

When The Clock Stopped 105

The Day The Ground Moved 106

A Day At The Lake 109

The Bike 114

Waiting 121

The Clock 122

Alone 125

Effervescent Potion 130

The Bonsai 136

Stranded 140

Author's Note 177

About the Author   179
EXCERPT FROM This Second Chance   180

IN THE TREE'S SHADOW

A collection of stories that exist in your dreams... and nightmares.

D. L. Finn

Also By D. L. Finn

Angels & Evildwels Series

This Second Chance (Book 1)

The Button: This Only Chance (Book 2)

This Last Chance (Book 3)

Companion Angels & Evildwels Stories

A Long Walk Home: A Christmas Novelette

Red Eyes in the Darkness: A Short Story

I Wouldn't Be Surprised: A Short Story

Paranormal Thriller

A Voice in the Silence

Short Story Collection

In the Tree's Shadow

Other Short Stories

Bigfoot: A Short Story

Poetry

Just Her Poetry Seasons of a Soul

No Fairy Tale: The Reality of a Girl Who Wasn't a Princess and Her Poetry
(Memoir)

Children's Books (middle-grade fiction)

Elizabeth's War (historical fiction)

An Unusual Island (fantasy)

Things on a Tree (holiday/fantasy)

Dolphin's Cave (fantasy)

Tree Fairies and Their Short Stories (fantasy)

Acknowledgments

I want to thank my amazing critique partners, Yvette and Patty—and my brilliant beta readers, Jan, Patty, Yvette, and Sandra! You are all such an important part of the writing process. Thank you to Denise at *Artful Editor* for making my words readable.

All my love goes to my husband, family, friends, and writing community, whose patient support and encouragement kept me going.

Finally to the readers, thank you for coming along for the ride! ☺

End Of The Road

My eyes blurred, jolting me from my trancelike state into reality. In the darkness before me, the two-lane highway beckoned me home. Its reflectors tapped in to my idle imagination. All I had to do was pull up on my steering wheel, and my car would take off like an airplane whose destination would be my private island away from it all. I could relax for those few seconds as I flew over the precipice. I was turning the steering wheel toward the cliff when a bright light blinded me. My foot slammed on the brake pedal. The car skidded to the side of the road in a cloud of dust as a feather landed on my windshield.

"What was that? A spaceship?" A shudder coursed through me. My heart pounded against my chest. I peered into the night. Nothing. The cliff was right next to me, bathed in the moonlight. I sucked in air, trying to make sense of what had happened. *Would I be at the bottom of the canyon if I hadn't seen that flash?*

Another white feather landed on my windshield. I hoped I was under a tree or utility line where a bird might be perched. I wasn't.

"Maybe an owl or . . . " I carefully got out of the car and retrieved the two feathers. It was me, my old Subaru, and the road. No alien invasion in sight. "I must be seeing things."

The cool air cleared my head. I didn't want to die, even if the thought had crossed my mind. I was *almost* entirely sure I wouldn't have done it. But I didn't have time to reflect on that as I studied the two white feathers in my hand. A message from the angels. Isn't that what my grandma used to say? She had told me solemnly to pay attention when I saw them unexpectedly.

"All right, I'm listening."

I slid back into the driver's seat and locked the door. I waited, but the night didn't offer anything new.

"Figures." I put the car in drive and headed home.

Even a miracle was as elusive as a successful diet. The six-hour round trip every week didn't help and filled me with anxiety. The worst part was that it didn't matter which direction I was going. At one end, a dying parent and the family's favorite sister fighting me on every decision about our alcoholic father. I had to be three steps ahead of her to protect the man who'd abused us. On the other end was a job I hated, a cat who avoided me, and my twin teenage boys, who were living with their father during their final year of high school. The cat and I had something in common—our loved ones had left us behind.

Being single grew on me in the same fashion as mold grows on shower grout. I kept trying to scrub it off, but it kept growing back. But if being solo was mold, then being in another dysfunctional relationship would be toxic mold. Besides, no one wanted to date a bitter, middle-aged, overweight woman with kids and a messed-up family, at least not in our small, upscale, ski resort town. Not that I had to worry about that since my schedule only allowed me to sleep, work, clean, do the British literature and biology homework that would put me one step closer to my master's degree and teaching certificate, and make this drive once a week.

I pulled into my pine tree–lined driveway with shame weighing me down. What had I been thinking? I wasn't living, only existing. The tidy brown contemporary house, which I'd had no say in selecting, didn't greet me. It was dark and forbidding. No surprise, my cat Frosty wasn't waiting for me in the front window. Still, I hoped he'd warm up to me someday. *Quit whining.* At least I had a roof over my head, a job, and two healthy kids—who lived with their financially thriving father.

"Too bad *my* dad isn't financially thriving."

To be honest, Dad's money was running out. Soon the only option left would be to sell his house to provide for his care, which he was entirely against. That reality seemed to fuel his desire to drink himself to death. Comfort care was the last step—making him as comfortable as possible. I felt the weight of the business card the hospice nurse had given me in my pocket. I was going to call in the morning.

"I don't want to end up like him," I told myself as I entered the frigid house, where I immediately dropped my purse on the floor and turned on the heater.

In our family, it came down to trust. Dad trusted my mom's terminal cancer would improve without all that doctor interference. All she needed to do was ask God for his forgiveness and send a hefty check to the man on TV. My mom trusted my drunken father and his lopsided beliefs. She would, not so delicately, tell me to mind my own business when I suggested she try some of the medical suggestions or at least get another opinion. Mom never got her forgiveness and died six months later.

My sister trusted all the wrong men. Three marriages had put her in debt and created an addiction to not only alcohol but substances from her doctor and drug dealers. She'd become a stranger to me, even though she claimed to be in recovery for the last six months. I didn't trust that or Dad's need to help her until he was broke. To continue the family trait, my blind devotion had gone to a man who said all the right things. Boy, did that backfire.

"Frosty!" I called out.

When I entered the kitchen, the spoiled orange cat didn't greet me, but stacks of dirty dishes and a basket of dirty clothes did. There was no relief in returning to a place that had lost its home status long ago. Now it was a place to stay until house prices increased and we could sell it. The profit would be shared between my undeserving, cheating ex-husband and me.

In the meantime, I had agreed to pay him half the mortgage payment while I lived in the house. I might have trusted the wrong divorce lawyer too. At least the boys came to stay with me every other weekend, and this was my weekend. I'd stay up late every night the week before their visit to get ahead on my homework so they could have my full attention.

The answering machine was blinking. I grinned, recognizing the number that came up when I pushed the button.

"Hey, Mom. Sammy and I are going to spend the weekend at Dad's cabin. We came and got Frosty to join us. Dad's missed him, and we didn't think you'd mind. Sorry we won't see you as planned, but Dad finished a big case, and we thought it might be the last time we could all hang out this summer. See you in two weeks. Love ya."

I moaned at the machine's hollow *click* and sank into the old blue rocker I had rocked the boys to sleep in as babies.

"Why did I bother coming back?"

I swiped away the tears filling my eyes, pushed myself up, and focused on cleaning the kitchen.

"I guess it's good for the boys to spend quality time with their dad." A fake cheerful voice emerged that didn't match my actions as I slammed the dishes into the dishwasher.

Heaven knows he wasn't there when they were growing up. I was. Now he could buy their affection. I couldn't compete with that. Each dish and bowl survived my anger, but the last glass did not. It shattered on the fake brick floor.

"Great." I grabbed the broom.

I thought life would turn out differently for me. When the boys went to college, I imagined Sam cutting back on his time at work. Things would go back to how they were before we had children. I would be part of his focus over work and golf—and later, his girl-friends.

I even caught him with one of those young women in our bed. She was the biggest cliché of all—his secretary. She had brought some papers by. He was alone, and things happened—by accident. Stupidly, I forgave him that first time after he explained it wouldn't have happened if I hadn't devoted all my time to raising toddlers. I apologized to *him,* if you can believe that. He bought me a massive diamond ring to signify our new start.

The second time, I saw his car parked at the local hotel. He insisted it was for work. Yes, I bought that too. He was an excellent lawyer. I give him that. Years passed, and I ignored the little things that warned me he wasn't a loyal husband.

I emptied the glass shards into the trash and uncharacteristically flung the broom on the floor. I took out the overflowing garbage—something my boys could have done for me when they picked up the cat but didn't.

At least I could take care of myself. The old Kelly of the past, who had been so naïve, was gone. I was no longer the girl who stayed home with the kids and dropped out of college because Sam didn't want his wife to work outside the home. I thought it would work because it was the opposite of what my mom had done. I was so youthfully confident that things would be great if I did things the right way, the opposite of what my parents did.

My reasoning needed to be revised. All that time, Sam said he was working overtime. He wasn't. This went on for fifteen years until he wanted his *space.* I was stunned. Then came a call from the latest girlfriend he'd met at the gym, Belinda. She didn't know about his family, she assured me. Belinda had already broken it off with him by the time he'd left me and moved on to the next woman's waiting arms.

Oddly enough, we became good friends. She's the one who helped me get a job and filled in the blanks of his past several years.

It took a long time to get to where I didn't regret my marriage, but only because of my boys. Plus, I developed that so-called backbone I'd been missing. Yes, it's made me more cynical, but the old doormat me still tries to make an occasional appearance.

"Ha!" My voice echoed hollowly as I lined the can with a fresh bag.

Then I poured myself a large glass of boxed white wine. A flash of light lit up my glass for a moment. A quick scan showed nothing was out of the ordinary, like on my ride home. I shook my head and finished my drink in three gulps. Maybe I needed to eat. I made a quick peanut butter sandwich and consumed it as enthusiastically as I poured the next glass of wine.

Responsible should have been my middle name for so many years. I've worked hard not to be that person anymore. I rolled my eyes at the laundry and ignored the empty refrigerator and stack of bills. Seeing a bright light on that stretch of highway broke something free that I had buried deep inside—me. My philosophical side awoke as I poured another glass of wine. Sanity and normalcy were over-rated was my conclusion.

Another flash of light came from the hall closet, and I dumped my full wineglass in the sink. Was I getting a migraine, or was it something else? I approached the closet with a kitchen knife in hand. Carefully peeking inside, I saw only years of living: board games, snow gear, a box of CDs, record albums, and my pink suitcase. Another feather landed on the luggage. I checked my pocket and found one of the two from the car.

"What's going on?" I asked the empty house.

Thankfully, there was no answer. I added a third feather to my growing collection. A smile crossed my face as I made a quick deci-sion. I filled the old suitcase from our honeymoon with shorts, tank tops, T-shirts, sweats, jeans, undergarments, and a bathing suit. I packed sunscreen and my e-reader, filled with books I wanted to read. With a smile, I added some PJs—not my comfortable ones, but the ones I've kept for a special occasion that never happened—and that dress I bought in case I needed something fancy. Maybe I'd need a coat too. I wasn't sure.

I crammed all my favorite clothes into the large suitcase. In a small bag, I added my makeup, cleanser, and creams. The rest of my toiletries fit inside the travel kit I had bought way back when but never used. On a whim, I grabbed the photo album of the boys growing up and a small box of pictures they'd drawn for me when they were little.

I glanced at my jewelry chest. My ex had gotten me some lovely pieces over the years. I should look my best. I stuffed them in my carry-on, along with the necklace my grandma gave me on my sixteenth birthday. A feather landed on the essential papers on my desk, and I added it to the ones already in my pocket. Maybe a bird was molting in the house. My full laugh filled the room. This was the most laughter it had heard since we moved in.

With a new spring in my step, I crammed those papers into my oversized purse, the one that my boys nicknamed "the suitcase." Relief flooded through me like an electrical current. I dialed my fully charged phone to call my job. I never missed a day, even when I was sick.

"I'm sorry, Dave. I won't be in on Monday. I quit."

I grinned. Next, I left a message at the hospice with instructions. I went on my laptop and stopped our—I mean *my*—newspaper and mail. I paid my bills and canceled the cable, electric, propane, and phone services. I made sure I had my car's pink slip in my purse and packed my laptop into its case. I was ready to go.

Sam loved the modern art in the beige-and-black living room—I considered it dull. It was devoid of the blues and greens I had always found soothing. I never wanted to see that room again. Dragging my luggage, I shut the door on my old life.

Feeling as light as the feathers I kept finding, I quickly maneuvered back onto the two-lane highway. I only stopped to get gas, pick up some snacks, and make my highest daily withdrawal possible. It comforted me that I'd accumulated the small savings printed on the receipt. I tucked it into my wallet next to my brand-new Visa with a $5,000 limit I had saved for emergencies. Today had become just that. Sam couldn't get a judge to order me to pay child support when the boys moved in with him last year, so there was no need to contact him further except to tell him to keep the cat and tend to the house.

My sister could take care of our childhood house—sell everything, for all I cared—and watch over Dad, or not, in hospice. I was done. I sent those texts and let Belinda know I was leaving town. I'd update her later. Then I shut off my phone.

When I got to the spot where I had seen that flash of light, I had the urge to pull back the car's steering wheel again, but this time to take off into my new life. I wanted to live. I always had. I had forgotten that. I had already wasted enough time taking care of a man who had abused me growing up, pining after a man who had left me, and raising boys who now were under the supervision of their father. Frosty was where he wanted to be. I was one semester away from becoming an English teacher. I could finish that online from anywhere. Yes, anywhere!

A highway patrol car drove by, and I checked my speed. I wasn't speeding, but his lights flashed on. I pulled over, and he kept going.

"That's all I would have needed after that wine! Kelly, you are out of your mind. You are running away from home. You're too old for that."

I smiled at myself in the rearview mirror. The face that looked back at me was happy, not out of her mind or even drunk. The green eyes were open with joy, the wrinkles weren't so bad, and the hair was still bottled blond. Maybe it was time to embrace the red hair Sam had never liked.

I didn't see the tramp my father had called me as a teenager or the lazy, boring, stay-at-home parent Sam had decided I was. There was no sign of that clingy woman who needed her man to care for her. I didn't want to become the woman my mother had been—old and bitter. I did not plan to die as she had. She'd seemed happy telling me she had cancer.

I looked down at my hands on the steering wheel. "No. You will not let that happen to you. You will be happy, starting with getting rid of this wedding ring."

I pulled it off, rolled down the window, and hesitated. I put it in my purse. *I should sell it.*

Three hours later, at 2:30 a.m., I ended up in front of my dad's house. It was dark because Dad was in the hospital until they set up hospice at home. My sister would be with her new guy, the same as every other controlling boyfriend she had ever had. I lost track of their names a while ago.

I wanted only one thing from that house, and my sister could have the rest, including my old car. My grandma had wanted me to have her bible, but my mother insisted it stay in her house. It was a book I had never seen her open, as much as she claimed to believe. Mom and I were never close like Grandma and I were. My mom wanted the bible because it meant she was important too. I understood that too late. On her deathbed, I forgave her. I will apply that to my abusive father and my ex-husband. The most important person to forgive was me. I deserved to be happy. I smiled as I unlocked the front door and stepped into the stale scent of cigarettes and whiskey.

The lights bathed the room that appeared the same as when I was a little girl. I had cleaned up my father's mess, but that didn't remove the heaviness the house held inside. I pulled my grandma's leather-bound bible from the top of the hall closet. I stroked the familiar book and smiled, remembering her reading from it daily. It reminded me of better times. When Grandma and Grandpa came over, Mom and Dad put on their "everything is just fine" act. I knew Grandma saw through that, but there was nothing she could do or say to change anything. She was the one who had been there for me until I lost her right before I got married. She was the only person who gave me unconditional love.

I sighed and turned on my mom's old computer. While it slowly

9

started, I made a strong cup of coffee and grabbed a handful of pistachios and a bag of barbecue chips. When the desktop loaded, I quickly booked a flight, found a ride, signed my pink slip, and turned the computer off. I left the pink slip on the kitchen counter with a note to my sister.

It's yours. I hope you find some happiness someday. It's never too late.

Then, with my bible in hand, I left my family home. Under the yellow glow of the porch light, I left my house key under the welcome mat, just where I told my sister I'd leave it. For the last time, my belongings and I drove away from the family house in an older black Mercedes with a taciturn Uber driver. I glanced back again as we turned onto the main road, leaving behind the street where I learned to hate myself.

The driver dropped me off at the airport around four. I'd never been to an airport at this hour. It was quiet. There were a few hours until my flight, so I tried to make myself comfortable in the uncomfortable blue vinyl chair by using my coat as a pillow and closing my eyes.

I was startled out of sleep when a briefcase slammed to the floor across from me. I studied the man in a dark suit, who pulled a newspaper in front of his pasty, stern face. Steam rose over the day's headlines. Coffee. That was what I needed.

I sat back down with my cup of wake up. The man didn't appear to have moved. The only thing different was his empty coffee cup on the yellow side table next to him. I picked up the bible. I wanted to read the words my grandmother had read to me as a child, but after I had untied and opened it, I didn't get that far. Inside were hundred-dollar bills tucked between pages.

"No way!"

The man looked up from his newspaper and sighed but didn't comment.

My grandma had told me she left something for me and then added, "Read the words." There were thousands of dollars. My parents had never looked inside. All this time, my sister had been stealing and this was right under her nose.

On the last page was a note:

Dearest Kelly,

I wish I were sitting next to you as you read this. I'm sure you're surprised at what I left you. It was the safest place to leave it. I knew no one else would look inside. You've grown into a beautiful woman, and I can only imagine the wonderful life you will have. Hang on to this for a few years. If life treats you well, then you won't need it. Maybe you could pass it on to your future kids. But don't give up if you ever find yourself in a spot as your mom did. I tried to help your mom, but she didn't want our help or anyone else's. She stayed in that horrible marriage and kept you kids in it too.

Use this to find the life you want if you don't have it. I hope I was wrong about Sam and he actually treats you well. Live your happily ever after. My days are limited, but know I'll watch over you and always love you.

XOXO

Grandma

A tear ran down my cheek. That confirmed everything I was doing right now.

"Flight 232 to Honolulu is boarding now at Gate 6."

It was six fifteen. The man behind the newspaper and I made our way to the gate. Because of the one person who had loved me unconditionally, I had enough to start over and come back and watch my boys graduate high school. This had turned into more than an escape. It was about creating a new life. I wasn't sure where I'd end up except sitting in the warm sun on a beach. I had an old male friend from high school who lived in Honolulu. He kept in contact, even though Sam had never approved of me having male friends. I would take him up on his invitation to stay in his guest room when I visited and then go from there. Maybe Belinda could come hang out with me. She had always talked of moving there too—the one place my ex refused to visit and I had always wanted to go.

I smirked, thinking about Sam's response and his sudden responsibilities with the house. When they graduated, the boys could visit anytime and spend the summer with me. Maybe they could go to college where I lived. You never know. It would be up to them, but for now, life was finally up to me, thanks to a feather, a flash of light, and a bible—gifts from the angels.

Old Gray Cat

Rupert, 2022
99 Words

THE OLD GRAY tux cat sits on the deck's wooden railing. His body's thin, but his fur is luxurious. He delicately sniffs the air, searching for his youth while observing the birds and butterflies. He's never been a hunter. The small animals he saved were in distress. He brought them to me with pure trust, knowing I'd try to save them. Today his green eyes reflect memories as he basks in the summer's sun. He knows what I know. The forest has a magic to offer. While his journey in my world might end, a new one awaits him.

The Playdate

For Jeff

I FORCED a smile and turned away from the picture. The yellow eyes were watching me. I nervously stuffed a cucumber sandwich into my dry mouth. Big mistake. It caught in my throat and then burned. I could taste the hot peppers as I coughed. I was positive I was going to die.

"Are you okay, Sandy?" Jessie's clear blue eyes showed concern as she handed me a glass of water.

"Yes, I swallowed wrong."

Bobby clung to my arm while Freddie sat on the couch, wearing a frown. This playdate was a huge mistake.

"Freddie, honey, why don't you show Bobby your room."

Freddie's face lit up. "Sure. I can show him my new ax!"

I cleared my throat. "Ax?"

"He asked for it for his birthday, but it's been put away. He knows we don't play with weapons when we have guests. Right, Freddie?"

Freddie let out a loud sigh. "Yes, Mommy. No weapons on playdates. I remember. But can we show him later?"

Jessie winked at me. "Maybe later."

I gently detached myself from Bobby's tightened grasp. "Maybe we should go with them."

"We'd be in the way." She waved. "You two be good."

Bobby followed Freddie down the hall like he was on death row making that last walk to his end. I was with him. They decorated the place like a haunted house, and the windows had dark drapes keeping the light and the world out. What wasn't black was gray, and the pictures! I shuddered. These were things of nightmares, including the so-called school picture of Freddie.

I sipped my water, trying to think of something to compliment in her house, but I drew a blank. "It's so kind of you to have us over. You didn't need to go to all this trouble with these sandwiches."

Jessie offered another one. "Please, help yourself."

"I didn't know we'd be eating. We just ate lunch, and I'm stuffed." I patted my stomach.

"I forgot to say something. My fault. Can I get you more water?"

I set my empty glass down. "No, I'm fine, thank you. So, are you an artist?"

Jessie set down the platter of little cucumber sandwiches. Her face brightened, and she clasped her hands together. "I am! I did all those photos and would love to make it into a business someday."

"Your own business. What a great idea." I jumped up and walked over to a wall covered with shots of Freddie. All had the same theme, him holding an ax in what looked like a torture chamber. "So, you take the pictures and then add the effects?"

"Oh, I never Photoshop a picture."

I held a frown behind my plastic smile. "You certainly have a way of capturing the shot."

Jessie squeezed next to me. "Thank you. Would you like to see my studio?"

I glanced at the old grandfather clock. Only fifteen minutes had passed since we had arrived. "Sure, I'd love to, but maybe we should check on the boys first."

"I say when it's quiet, you leave them alone, right?"

Against my better judgment, I nodded. She led me down a dark hall into a lightless room and flipped on a light.

I gasped.

"I know, isn't it wonderful? I've got it just the way I want it."

"Wonderful," I mumbled, taking in the horror.

The walls and ceiling were black, and two round lights on a stand looked like angry headlights waiting to shine on their victim. A rounded black chair was pushed against the gloom, while off to the side was an assortment of black clothes and props that included hands, legs, guns, knives, axes, and a guillotine. The farthest wall had metal shackles. A potent scent of copper hit my nose as pain tore through my gut. I needed to get Bobby out of this madhouse.

Jessie smiled and put a hand on my shoulder. "That will pass."

The room spun as I sank to the floor. "What?"

"Your humanness, silly. What I put in your water is returning you to your beautiful form. I tried to make it easier by showing you the pictures of Freddie and my studio."

My muscles spasmed like a seizure, and suddenly the room was too bright. I closed my eyes.

"I'll get the light. Earth is bright for us. You'll stay here until the ship arrives. That way, you won't have to wear all that makeup and those contacts and worry about the sun damage."

When the spasms stopped, it all came flooding back to me. I volunteered for this. I secured a relationship with and then married a top-ranked government employee. They could extract the important secrets from my brain implant during my sleep cycles. Of course, Bobby wasn't supposed to happen, and the poor thing would have to live with the shame of being part human. I reached up and stroked my leathery face. I was back.

"Feeling better?" Jessie wiped off the rest of her makeup and popped out her contacts. It was a relief to take in the beautiful deep red around her yellow eyes and almost-transparent white skin.

"Yes, much. Is Bobby . . . " I couldn't find the words to ask.

Jessie smiled. "He looks like us, thankfully. However, we had to give the poor baby the human drug immediately after birth and adjust some memories. But that doesn't matter now that he's back in his true form. Freddie knows how to help him during the change, don't worry. Nothing can pierce his skin now—like those old axes. I'm sure they're having a lot of fun."

I grinned. "Thank you, Jessie. When does it all start?"

"In a week. We are gathering our spies and have all the necessary information to simplify it. This planet will make a great second home once humans have been rendered docile for our food supply. We found the perfect virus that won't affect us, thanks to you. Our alliance appreciates your service."

I straightened up, slowly finding my balance again. "Thank you. It was an honor. I'm glad you could continue your artwork—the humans must have made great subjects."

She smiled brightly. Her pointed teeth shone like stars. "Yes. Their surprised look when they realized what was about to happen was the best. Let's get the boys and have a nice snack. Too bad no one will get their mail today."

I laughed and swayed my tail. "Great! I'm hungry."

It was good to feel myself again, and I couldn't wait to return home. Bobby had a new world to explore, where beautiful darkness ruled.

It's Only A Dream

Based on the Angels & Evildwels Series

ZELINA THE ANGEL stood by Lisa's side in the darkness. Lisa's quivering body was bathed in sweat as she pulled on her green robe and headed to the kitchen. Zelina regretted the dream that had terrified her, but there was no other way to warn her. Would it be enough? She hoped it would be.

Zelina wasn't the only one there with her. Evil was there too.

Lisa's hands trembled as she poured the boiling water into her favorite rose china teacup over a bag of Earl Gray. The citrus smell calmed her racing pulse but didn't push away the nightmare's images. That terrifying dream was back, with a new ending. It started with her in the middle of an unfamiliar forest. She was surrounded by blowing snowdrifts. As the storm raged on, she trudged through knee-deep snow. The trees thinned ahead, and she stepped into a clearing where light beckoned from a log cabin.

The house drew her like a magnet. She needed to know what was inside for no logical reason. The snow stopped falling, and the plummeting temperatures seeped through her snow gear. Her boots crunched loudly in the frozen snow instead of sinking into it as they had in the forest. The steps of the wraparound porch were free of snow. A wooden bench draped in a neatly folded red plaid blanket and a matching rocking chair showed the owners liked to relax outside. A statue of an angel reading to a small child stood on a small stone table. It made Lisa smile.

She approached the stunning wooden door with a mother bear and two cubs carved into it. *This is a door I'd love to have gracing my entry.*

She grasped the silver knocker with her gloved hand and knocked twice without response. A chill shot up her spine, and her curiosity turned into concern. She pushed the door open with a loud creak.

"Hello? Is anyone home?"

No answer as she wiped her feet on the bear welcome mat and stepped inside. Just ahead was her dream kitchen, glimmering with new stainless steel appliances, a fireplace, and a white farmhouse table. The house was cozy and welcoming, yet the urge to escape nudged her.

"Hello?"

Four steps in, the entry opened into a huge family room—and death.

"Oh, no!"

Lisa froze, but her body was fully alert as she took it all in. Dark blood flowed out in all directions across the beige carpet like a malicious flower growing from the two adults and two children. No one moved. The father's right hand still grasped a gun. Pulling off her glove, she rushed to check their pulses, starting with the children. Her fingers met cold skin and four lifeless bodies.

This can't be happening. She backed away from the empty blue eyes of the boy, who had to be around seven years old. His cowlick and freckles reminded her of her younger brother.

She turned away as her stomach heaved. The large brown-haired man lay face down next to his wife. The mother still clasped the Spiderman PJ top of the youngest, while the older boy was several feet away from his family, as if he'd tried to escape. Thankfully, she could see only one face, but that image would haunt her forever.

She carefully picked up the gun. The metal was heavy in her hand, and she found one bullet in the chamber. Her stomach settled, and she set the murder weapon down. She gently covered the family with a large blue blanket draped over the couch.

What if the killer is still here? With renewed urgency, she picked up the gun and searched the house.

Her snow boots echoed off the wooden floor, and she narrowly missed tripping over a baseball bat. She picked up the wooden bat as tears flowed. Quietly sobbing, she checked the three bedrooms, closets, bathroom, and laundry room. Each room, filled with loving details of family memories, sent a stab of pain through her heart. She was the only one alive. She dropped the gun and bat by the bodies.

There was nothing else she could do. She averted her gaze as she passed by the family with a frantic hope that they would be sitting on the couch sipping hot chocolate instead. Her wish wasn't granted, and she turned her attention to the father. Was he the killer or the protector? Was he the one who woke his family up and—no, she couldn't think about that.

Numbness flowed over her. The scent of the wilting red roses in a square vase centered on the kitchen table and the wood half-consumed in the icy stove filled her with heavy sorrow. She shivered. Why weren't the windows covered in frost? She looked for a sign to guide her, but all hope had been extinguished. Carefully she made her way past the grisly scene to the old-fashioned white wall phone.

This isn't real. This is a dream, she tried to remind herself.

Yet that knowledge didn't stop her heart pounding as she wiped away her tears. She picked up the receiver and punched 9-1-1.

"I'd like to report a murder."

Her voice responded to the questions like she was observing herself on a crime TV show.

"No, the entire family is dead. I checked. . . . Yes, all four of them. . . . No, I didn't see anyone else, but I found a gun. I kept it until I knew I was safe. I think they were killed—unless it's a murder-suicide. . . . Yes, but you aren't here."

The woman's voice was calm on the other end of the line. "Take a deep breath. Ma'am, help is on the way. We won't know what happened until we arrive. Now, can you tell us why you are there? Are they friends of yours?"

Lisa didn't know how to respond and hung up.

This is just a dream.

She stepped outside. Dark, menacing clouds covered the sun. Instead of returning to the forest, she sank into the wooden rocking chair with a loud sigh that melted into the quiet grove of pines.

She slowly rocked, as that mother had probably done many times with her boys. Tiny flakes drifted from the sky to add to the white landscape. The only color in the winter gloom was a flash of blue lights in the distance. Her mind began to process what she'd seen.

Although her observations suggested that the father had shot himself in the head, something was troubling her. Was it meant to look like that? Not that she had any experience with dead bodies— outside this dream, she'd never been around one. She waited for the dream to end where it always did, but this time, it didn't.

She took a long drag of a cigarette that had turned up in her right hand. Even though she had quit ten years ago, the smoke soothed her. She continued sucking in the calming vapor while the SUV rushed to her aid, lights blazing.

It skidded to a halt. Two men exited the vehicle with guns drawn. The older one stood at least six foot five.

"Put your hands up where we can see them," he warned.

She complied as the younger man retrieved the gun. The next thing she knew, she was in the back of the SUV.

"Don't worry, ma'am. This is a murder-suicide," said the older officer. He had coffee breath and lousy posture. "I never thought he'd be capable of this. They always seemed like the perfect family. Never know, I guess."

Lisa hugged herself tightly. "What if it wasn't the father?"

"Unlikely, ma'am." The younger partner shook his head, making a single brown curl bounce against a prominent ear.

No one asked for her name, and she didn't know theirs.

They drove away from the log cabin with the windshield wipers pushing the falling snow to the side. Lisa glanced through the SUV's back window and studied the house. Such a beautiful house, in such a pretty place. Such a shame. At the edge of the trees, a man with white, wild hair, wearing a bright red scarf, glared at her with glowing red eyes. He waved.

"Stop! I see someone."

"Where?" The officer slammed the brakes, jerking her forward against her seat belt with an *oomph*.

"Behind that tree!" She pointed to the spot where the man had retreated into the trees.

"You mean in that big Douglas fir grove?"

"Yes."

"We'll check the area. You wait here." A sly glance passed between the two men. They didn't believe her.

She sighed as they searched for him. The killer was watching them—she could feel it. They weren't gone long before they climbed back into the SUV.

"We didn't see anyone or any tracks in the snow. It must have been a shadow."

"I saw him." Lisa frowned.

"You're upset. Eyes can play tricks on you."

Lisa glanced outside. As they pulled away, the red-eyed killer emerged from the trees laughing. A large black bear stood beside him. This time, she didn't bother to tell them. He would hide again, and they'd insist it was a bear.

The dream ended. She'd finally seen the killer, and it hadn't been the father. It was a monster.

Lisa shook her head. *What did the new dream ending mean?* She could predict what her therapist would say. "The dream represents your childhood. And with your parents dying five years ago, it makes sense that you'd dream about it again. Since that dead family embodies your family growing up, seeing the killer waving to you shows you've made peace and are moving on with your life. How does it make you feel to have closure?"

So why bother making an appointment if she knew what would be said? Not that the therapist was wrong. She had been thinking about her parents' car accident. They died not from gunshots but shots of tequila. Their drinking had killed her childhood and that of her younger brother. The day her parents died, he moved away and started a life that didn't include her or his past.

Maybe she did get her closure. She was relieved it wasn't the father who killed his family. Perhaps it was over for her now that she had identified the killer and forgiven her parents, especially her father, who had been driving the night her parents crashed into a tree. They had been killed instantly. And she had had a wonderful life with her amazing husband and daughters in a yellow Victorian-style house nestled in the forest on seven acres, like Sleeping Beauty's cottage with the fairies. Lisa refused to let a nightmare control where she lived.

She returned to writing as the morning's light slowly filtered through the trees. With shoulders squared, a hard-boiled egg in one hand, hot tea in another, and her laptop tucked under her arm, Lisa headed for her favorite spot on the front porch, where she wrote in the peace of sunrise before her family got up. These quiet moments brought her so much joy. This fantasy world was a great place to escape when her memories or nightmares threatened to interfere with her happily ever after in real life.

The words wouldn't come. Instead, she sat in the silence of the winter's dawn, wrapped in her blue blanket, and sipped her tea.

Those red eyes haunted her. She sighed loudly, pushing that memory away. Her story could wait. Poetry always helped her work through her problems or worries.

darkness birthed morning
a glowing light reached shadows
but not the evil

She wrote more senryus, haikus, and free verse until that evil darkness faded away and all that was left was peace and beauty. As the sun rose higher in the sky, she added another chapter to her children's fantasy. She hit save when tiny feet raced down the hardwood floor of the hall to the family room.

Zoey and Zella, her sweet seven-year-old twin girls, would eat breakfast with their dad. Usually they wouldn't disturb her until Mark left for work and took them to school. Then she'd do her paying job, editing other people's books. But this morning, Mark didn't have to go to work, and the girls didn't have school during the holiday break.

Intensely craving a cigarette for the first time in years, she added one more poem to her journal. Deep inside, a voice took over, and the last line became a warning: *Evil is coming.*

She buried that negative voice and closed her laptop. She carefully folded the soft blanket and laid it on the back of the bench. Snowflakes tumbled down as she headed back inside to be embraced by a strong whiff of cinnamon. She pasted on a bright smile for Mark as he presented her with pancakes shaped like Mickey Mouse and the girls threw their arms around her. Everything tipped back to normal. Soon they were dressed to play in the snow.

While the girl's eager voices sang about building a snowman and the sky gave them more than enough snow for their creations, the darkness slithered back. She squinted and studied the tree line. What was out there?

Guess writing out the bad in poetry didn't work this time. She shook her head and returned her attention to her family. Lisa's perfect day ended around the fireplace, watching her girls' favorite movie, *Sleeping Beauty,* as she dozed off.

* * *

Zelina frowned and stretched out her peacock-green wings. "It is time."

Ed, a human spirit who assisted the angel, ran his hand through his hair and massaged his scalp. "Why do you keep sending her that dream? How will that help her now?"

Zelina raised an eyebrow at him. "She has seen the killer and the hint of what is inside him. Maybe if she is aware, she will act. See him?"

"Yes."

"This evildwel chose a cruel human to live in to feed off the pain he causes."

Ed shook his head. He wished he had wings, like Zelina. "No one will know the truth if we can't stop this creep."

"I know, but her brother, who keeps track of her life, will see what she wrote. Even if the outcome cannot be changed, he will know how her dream ended. Tyler will not believe the conclusion the police arrive at."

"Mark wanted a gun, and Lisa wouldn't allow one in their house. They have no protection. Now what? They should leave." Ed rubbed his hands together. He never understood how a spirit still experienced the cold even without a nervous system.

Zelina frowned deeply. "A gun would not matter here. And this killer will wait. He is patient."

Ed threw his hands out. "Why them?"

Zelina put a hand on his arm with a sad smile. "She smiled at him once. He hated that. That was all it took."

"Are you kidding me?"

Zelina put her delicate but powerful hands on her hips. "I certainly am not."

Ed's feet left no tracks in the snow, but he sure felt the cold. "Why do you need my help with this? It seems like there's nothing we can do. Bad is going to happen here."

"That is never a given, especially with an evildwel and when good is involved."

"Those black, misty leeches. I hate those things. Feeding off human fear like one did with me before you saved me and offered me a second chance. I wish they didn't exist."

Zelina spoke softly. "But they do, and so do we."

"You want me to try, Zelina?" Ed met her intense gaze.

"Of course I do. I hope you can separate the evildwel from its host, and it will leave. Then it will just be the host they are dealing with. Might offer them a slim chance of survival if all goes well."

"What aren't you telling me?" Ed folded his arms.

Zelina shook her head. "You know me too well, my friend. We have been through this before. There is another evildwel nearby. It is not using a human as a host. I do not know what it wants unless it is waiting to feed, and then more might gather for that. If they figure out how to work together, it could be impossible to fight them."

"Great."

The angel turned away. "No, it is not."

"I know. I was being sarcastic."

"Yes, I know. I have dealt with your humor since we saved your ex-wife and kids. I was grateful when you separated that evildwel from your son. It was a miracle. Have you checked on your family recently? Your grandchild is growing up so fast."

Ed noted her change of subject. She always held something back from him, but he let it pass. "Yes, I watch them in between our assignments. I'm so proud of them, yet I had nothing to do with their success. Rachael did," he said with a slight shrug.

"I am proud of your growth. You can take credit for that."

"Thanks, but it was overdue after how I treated my family when I was alive. But what about now? What can we do to stop this slaughter? Or are we winging it like always?

"Yes, wings come in handy." Zelina smiled and winked before allowing the back-to-business expression to take charge.

Ed pointed. "Maybe I'll go talk with the lurking evildwel. Let him know it's time to leave."

"Wait." Zelina held up her hand.

"I'm always careful around these misty monsters." Ed pinned his gaze on the man creeping through the silent house.

"I know, but we have run out of time. There will be no talking. You must act now."

"Separation time, misty monster." Ed headed to the living room.

The man with the cruel smile and wild white hair was inches above Lisa's sleeping figure. Without a second thought, Ed jumped and landed inside the man. The dark mist swirled around him while the pain gripped his attention. A heaviness took over, and Ed couldn't move, his mouth open in a silent scream.

Ed used every ounce of willpower to meet the red eyes before him. He could feel the strength of this evildwel. It would be a challenge to separate him from his human host. Not that it mattered. This man, without his evildwel, might still kill this family, but at least this creature couldn't feed off their fear. Maybe the family had a slight chance of fighting off the man, but they couldn't survive a man with an evildwel inside.

Ed tore his eyes away and sighed. There was the other evildwel hidden in a dark corner. It didn't appear to want to help, just feed. Zelina's worries weren't coming to pass about them working together this time. He slowly advanced into the heart of the darkness. Each step was more painful than the last.

He had to meet it on its terms and send it love, the only thing that repelled them and might remove this one from its host. Each battle to remove an evildwel felt like he was dying, which was ironic because he was already dead.

The human host's attention turned back to those beautiful little girls, and he headed down the hall. Ed wasn't going to let him hurt them. He had to stop him one way or another.

Lisa snuggled closer to Mark as she half-listened to the last words of the movie the girls had watched for the fifth time in a row. She knew the dialogue by heart, and a small smile crossed her face. She had peacefully fallen asleep with Mark holding the girls next to him. But fear tugged at her slumber and woke her up. The girls weren't next to Mark. They must have gone to bed on their own, which they often did. Mark quietly snored, so she untangled herself and went down the hall.

She peeked into Zella's room. Her red hair was the only thing sticking out under her new pink fairy comforter. Lisa smiled and stealthily advanced to check on Zoey. The warm glow of a fairy nightlight pulsated from the room. Lisa peered inside, expecting brown hair sticking out from under a blue fairy comforter. Instead, a man was standing over her daughter holding a gun. Her breath got stuck in her throat, and she held back her fury.

Lisa pulled back, hidden from his view. She was sure he hadn't seen her but worried he could hear her pounding heart trying to explode out of her chest. There was no time to wake up Mark, and the element of surprise was her only hope. Had her dream been about them the whole time? It didn't matter now. All she could do was find something to use as a weapon to protect her family. She refused to let them end up like that poor family from her dreams.

Her gaze was pulled to the bear picture at the end of the hall. The bear! Right next to it was the closet, her husband's old bat and glove inside. Luckily, the door wasn't shut, thanks to Mark's habit of never fully closing drawers or shutting doors. She crept to the closet, grabbed the bat and cradled it as she had in her dream, and crept back to the door, inch by inch. She closed in on him.

What if this is a trap? There was no time to second-guess. She slowly lifted her arms and positioned herself to swing at his head when a dark mist exploded from the man. Red eyes glared at her as it floated away. *What was that thing?*

The man continued smiling down at her daughter without moving. Then he shook his head as if to clear it and bobbled the gun, almost dropping it. Lisa pushed away what she'd seen and repressed the scream inside as she swung the bat. It connected loudly with the back of his skull. As he sank to his knees, the gun went off, and she felt a sharp sting cut through her upper arm.

A nauseous wave rolled through her, but she had to get that gun from him. Dropping the bat, she grabbed the gun, but his grasp held firm. Her daughter's brown eyes were wide with horror as Mark yelled her name. Everything moved in slow motion. Both of their hands were on the gun, but it was pointed at her. An older man, he was much stronger than he looked. His steel-gray eyes bore into hers. She had only hurt him, and now his attention was on her demise.

"Mommy!" Zoey cried out as tears ran down her face.

He smiled, yanked the gun away, and turned it on her daughter. She threw herself on his arm as the gun went off again. It missed Zoey—narrowly.

Mark burst into the room as the man grinned and shook his head again. He looked more like he could play Santa than Satan. He pointed the gun at Mark, who jumped out of the way when it went off. Zella screamed from her room.

"Get his gun!" Mark yelled.

"Not going to happen, sir. Your end has begun." The man spoke as one would to a small child.

It was chilling how normal he sounded. How polite. He pulled away from Lisa, the gun still pointed at Zoey.

"Lock your door, Zella!" Lisa cried.

She had failed her family, and now they were going to die.

A sudden beam of light that reminded her of a flashlight bounced off a wall and hit the man in the eyes. It appeared to blind him for a moment. This was her only chance. She lowered her head and rammed it into his knees. An older guy had to have bad knees.

That sickening clash of head and kneecap caused the killer to gasp, giving Mark enough time to take him down. The gun went off one more time, and it went through the arm that had already been hit. The pain would have floored her at any other time, but she was focused on saving her family. The gun dropped like a crashing plane and landed next to a police badge. It all became clear—the killer was a cop. She scooped up the weapon with her good hand and sat on her daughter's bed.

"Mommy, you have a boo-boo." Zoey was scrunched up in the corner with her fairy comforter. She sniffled and wiped her tear-stained face with her PJ sleeve.

Lisa looked down. Her arm was bleeding in two places, but it didn't feel life-threatening. She grabbed her daughter's discarded pants and tied them over her wounds.

"I'm sorry the bad man scared us, but you're safe now. Daddy is taking care of him. Would you go make sure your sister's okay, honey?"

Zoey sat up, letting the blanket fall away. "What was that dark thing, Mommy?" she asked in a small voice.

Lisa forced a smile as a chill raced through her. "I saw that too. It was a reflection from the hall. Go to your sister, and I'll be right in."

"Okay, Mommy." Zoey hugged her before she raced out of the room without looking at the man.

Lisa shook her head grimly. "If I were stronger, I could have knocked him out."

"That head butt did the job." Mark landed a heavy punch in the face of the wriggling man. He stopped moving and appeared to be passed out. Mark kneeled and grasped his arms.

Lisa nodded and fixed her makeshift bandage.

Mark tried to make a lame joke. "I hope he's the only serial killer cop on the force."

Lisa sighed. "Too soon."

"Sorry." He shrugged.

"I'll call the police, check on the girls, and get the duct tape for him."

"You're hurt. I'll do it. Keep that gun pointed at him."

She sat on her daughter's bed as a wave of exhaustion rolled over her. Mark moved toward her and wrapped her in a quick hug. "Keep that arm still."

Lisa's eyes were heavy, but she shook her head to wake up. It jolted her arm, sending pain through her body. She was fully awake as she clenched the gun on the unmoving man.

"They're on their way," Mark announced, holding up the tape. "Your dream—do you think it was a warning?"

"I think so."

"You were so brave." Mark towered over the man, who now looked frail.

Lisa shook her head. "Not brave, scared for my family. It could have gone either way."

Mark secured the man's wrists with a generous amount of tape. "The bat was in your dream."

Lisa slowly found her footing, careful to keep her arm still. "And bears. Maybe I thought of the bat in the closet because of the picture."

Mark kissed her cheek as they stood over the man. "I think he's coming to."

"Here's the gun. I'm gonna get a towel and then stay with the girls. Make sure you tape his mouth. I don't want to hear a word he has to say."

Mark smiled. "Done."

After she tended to her wounds, Lisa found her girls huddled together in Zella's room. She carefully scooped them both into a hug and kissed them. "I know that was scary, but you're okay now."

Zella nodded and smiled. "We know, Mommy. The pretty lady and funny man stayed with us."

"Pretty lady and funny man?" Lisa repeated.

"Yes. She had wings like my fairies. They said we were safe now. Do you want to meet them?"

"Yes, I would love to meet them." Lisa played along.

Zella looked around. "Hey, where did they go?"

"It's okay. They said goodbye, remember?" Zoey said.

Zella nodded firmly. "Oh yeah, they did."

Lisa smiled. "Well, I'd like to thank them for keeping you safe."

Zoey grasped her mom's hand. "The man wasn't a fairy, but he got rid of that black cloud thing. He helps fairies."

Lisa shivered. "Sounds like you're talking about an angel, girls. We—"

Zoey didn't let her finish. "Mommy, will you read to us if we hold the book for you?"

They spent some quiet time reading their favorite fairy book while Mark watched over the killer in the other room. Soon there was a knock at the front door.

"That's the police. Come on, girls."

They hurried to answer the door. A man and a younger woman entered the house with their guns drawn, except they looked nothing like the police in her dream. After introductions, Lisa quickly explained what had happened. They hurried inside Zoey's bedroom to find one of their own on the floor.

Lisa stayed at the door, blocking the girl's view. They were none too gentle cuffing the man as Officer Clair read him his rights, and they didn't remove the pink tape from his mouth. Soon he was out of their house.

Officer Clair returned to the house while her partner, Randy, stayed with the suspect. She put a hand on Lisa's shoulder. "An ambulance will be here soon, ma'am." A bright smile crossed her face as she looked down at the girls. "They will fix your brave mommy up."

Zella's eyes widened. "Could we go in the ambulance too?"

Lisa shook her head. "Maybe next time, girls. You can stay with Daddy."

Officer Clair patted the top of Zella's head with a smile that lit up her eyes, making them look like emeralds. "I recommend you all get checked out to be safe."

Lisa nodded. "That may be a good idea, but thankfully, no one else was hurt. I can't believe a local officer is a killer."

Officer Clair sighed loudly. "Oliver Diaz worked on the force for twenty years before he retired last year. He always seemed so nice—too nice. No one ever connected the murder cases he worked on to him. We'll have to reexamine every case he had. We're sorry we missed this, but not as sorry as he'll be when he goes to jail."

Officer Clair's phone beeped. "Even chained up, the ambulance can't make it over that last hill to get here. Will your truck make it out of here? You can follow us. We don't want to put you with the prisoner."

"I've driven in worse," Mark said. He closed Zoey's bedroom door. "I'll get the girls dressed and meet you out there."

Officer Clair looked around the house, nodded, and left.

Lisa slipped into her snow boots, wrapped a blanket around herself, grabbed her purse, and shut off the lights. Soon they were in the truck heading to the hospital, where she only required some stitches and cleaning up. Both bullets had exited cleanly, missing the bones and anything important. The doctor told her more than once how lucky she was. Everyone checked out fine, including the killer. Lisa finally understood why she'd had the dream—which had nothing to do with her childhood, as her therapist had thought. It had been a warning, showing her how to protect her family. She was thankful for that.

* * *

Zelina and Ed watched from a corner of the hospital room.

"Thanks for removing another evildwel, Ed. That made the difference and gave her the perfect time to use that bat."

"My pleasure! Nice touch with the beam of light."

Zelina nodded. "We do what we can."

"Another happy ending, huh, Zelina?"

"It sure is."

Ed winked. "I'm a big fan of those. I'm getting sentimental in my older—well, whatever age I am now."

Zelina grinned, "Me too, my friend. Me too."

A Reminder

99 Words

STELLA SAT on the old wooden porch swing and gently rocked. Birds sang their sweet song while the forest swayed to the music: nothing to do and no place to go. The clouds formed shapes that summer afternoon. Day faded into the pink-and-purple splendor when light caressed the darkness. That moment birthed the first joy she'd felt since her days of busyness and usefulness, when the world had respected her worth. Today she was reminded of her quiet love of nature. The natural world loved her back by awakening her wonder and opening her poetic door—a new beginning.

A Man On The Pier

THE LANKY APPARITION known as Captain Randall carried a long cage full of dead fish in his arms along a wooden pier. He was dressed in brown pants and a blue shirt with brass buttons. His stringy gray hair was tied back with a strip of tanned leather, and his brown boots were scuffed and worn. He set his contraption across from where I sat on the newly painted white bench.

Nothing would have happened that day if it hadn't been for that man out jogging.

The runner in gray sweats and a shiny blue fitted shirt skidded to a stop in front of Captain Randall, who looked like any other fisherman except for his dated clothes. I jumped up to stop him, but he said, "Hi, I'm Lucas, and I'm new to the area. What's that for?"

Captain Randall smiled, exposing a mouthful of rotten teeth as he skillfully sliced open the rotting fish. "Come see, Lucas. Follow me." He gripped the cage and jumped into the icy waters.

I grasped Lucas's sweaty arm, shaking my head. He grinned, pushed me away, and followed the captain into the water without hesitation.

"Hey! What are you doing?" Lucas called out as he swam faster.

I froze at the edge of safety and watched them swim away from the pier. My heart raced like I was doing laps at the high school pool. That's where I had spent most of my free time in those days—I was team captain in my senior year. Right now, though, I didn't want to cross a finish line. I longed to be in that water. It took every ounce of my willpower not to jump in or shout out to Lucas to come back. If I did either, that would be my demise too.

The long cage was opened, and the dead fish floated on top of the ocean water. Blood seeped out, coating the surface with death. Captain Randall swam back to the pier dragging the empty cage behind him.

Lucas looked around with his mouth hanging open. I knew what was about to happen. I had been warned since childhood not to speak around this ghost by the adults in my life and my dreams. There was nothing I could do.

Captain Randall turned when he got to the pier. Lucas's eyes widened as black fins appeared on either side.

"Help me!" Lucas's hands waved frantically in the air.

Captain Randall calmly climbed out of the ocean. There was no helping Lucas—he disappeared under the blood-red sea in one giant wrench.

Captain Randall nodded to me. "Guess they're biting today."

I gulped down any response.

With a slight smile, he walked off, humming a tune that sounded like the theme from that shark movie. I watched the water become inflamed with death.

My stomach clenched as my dream replayed in my head. "Never, never speak to him. He's cursed, Sasha," a beautiful woman with long black hair and a fish's body for legs had warned. "Stay out of the water, no matter what you see. Someday I will return for you."

Too bad no one told Lucas that the ghost of Captain Randall fed the sharks every day at the same time. If you were foolish enough to speak to or around him and he responded, your fate was sealed.

The frenzy only continued for a few minutes.

I wasn't shocked when the mermaid from my dream swam up to the pier's edge after the waters cleared to their usual crystal-blue beauty.

"That's the evil we battle, Sasha. It didn't recognize who you were. I'm pleased. Now go back to your land home until you're needed."

"You battle evil? Why would it recognize me?"

"When it's time, I will come for you and explain. Go back." She disappeared.

That was three years ago. I moved to the city and have yet to return to that pier or the ocean. Thankfully, there've been no more dreams. The only water I ever got into was full of chlorine. But that all changed last night when the images returned to my sleep, calling me to the sea. Wide awake, I foolishly went down to do laps in the pool at my apartment building. It was early, and the pool was usually empty. I set my towel on a blue lounge. I stood on the edge, ready to dive, when a mermaid appeared. She waved, and I ran.

No one can make me go back to the sea again. I won't. Even when I ran past Captain Randall carrying his fish in the middle of my apartment lobby, I convinced myself it had nothing to do with me. I threw my clothes and some personal items into my new green suitcase and left behind the shabbily furnished studio apartment and my server job. I'm still running a year later, but I'm called back to the sea in my sleep. I'm no mermaid. Nothing will trick or fool me into returning to any body of water. Ever. I learned strength growing up in the foster care system.

With no place to go, I moved to the desert. The dreams continue, but let those water people try to find me here in all that dry sand. Just let them.

In The Shadows

I SAVED my work and turned off the laptop. Lucy, my devoted German shepherd, waited patiently for me to put on my shoes and tug on my warm coat and mittens. Stepping outside, I shivered and zipped up my coat as Lucy pushed past into the lead. The late afternoon sunbeams filtered through the pines and offered no warmth, but I found joy in the trees that glowed with autumn's jewels.

It was my favorite time of year—the heat of summer was a distant memory, and winter's chill hadn't taken hold. Yet today it was different. As I stepped off the redwood deck, unease settled over me like I was being watched. I scanned the silent tree-lined perimeter, but I saw nothing unusual as Lucy sprinted to our walking trail. I quickened my pace, unable to shake off that disturbing sensation. Lucy's piercing bark mixed with a gray squirrel's loud chirp of displeasure as the small rodent raced up a cedar, sending chunks of bark flying.

"Just a squirrel," I said, more to myself than Lucy.

I'd been jumpy lately. Well, more than normal. Living alone had always suited me, but recently it seemed as if my safe place in the woods was being invaded by the craziness I had long avoided. I brushed those feelings aside because I had work to do and books to write. I was a best-selling horror author with deadlines. I might write about scary things, but I knew ghosts and monsters weren't real. They were just the way I made a living.

What was real was enjoying my plot of soil in the forest and supporting my peaceful lifestyle in the fashion I had become accustomed to. Marriages hadn't worked out. Yes, having someone to share my work and moments with was nice, but they always wanted more than that. More than I could give. I'd been content for five years since my last messy breakup.

Animals were there for me in the ways I needed, while humans required too much. I was comfortable with Lucy for now after the painful loss of my kitty to cancer last year. My pets were my family, and now it was just Lucy and me.

The brown, yellow, and red leaves crackled under my tennis shoes. I kicked a pile that scattered across my path. I had no intention of raking up those autumn leaves from the mowed weeds I called a lawn.

The feeling of being watched increased, and I shuddered. The squirrel had gone silent, and Lucy waited for me.

"Good girl." I stroked her black-and-tan fur.

We walked silently along the dirt trail into the forest. I breathed in the musty scent of the trees and bathed in their wisdom. My shoulders relaxed, and I let my cares float beyond the tree line. Here, I released my writing world for my real world. Clouds passed overhead as we went deeper into the long shadows.

Thunder rumbled, stripping away my serenity. I quickened my pace.

"The storm wasn't supposed to come until after midnight."

Lucy wagged her tail and drew closer to me. I smiled at her reassuringly, but that didn't fool her. The impending thunderstorm was a concern, but so was whatever was in the shadows.

"Let's go home, Lucy, before we get struck by lightning."

I turned quickly when something snapped to our left. Lucy growled, looking in the noise's direction.

My heart sped up as my shaking hands clipped her green leash to her pink leather collar. "No, Lucy, it's probably a deer or bear. You can't chase it."

I tried to tug her back toward home, but she wouldn't budge. I would not win this battle with my stubborn 125-pound dog.

"Lucy," I warned. "Come on! Let's go!"

Finally she turned her head to me, but her tail was curled under and her hackles raised. The hair on my arms matched hers. We hurried back toward the house as the first raindrops soaked into the dry fall ground.

Another snap and then a deep laugh.

"Who's there?" I called out.

There was no response. Lucy's rumbling bark echoed through the forest.

"Shh, it's okay, girl," I whispered. "Come on, probably some teenagers."

A rock landed near me, and I jumped.

"You're trespassing. I'm going to call the police," I warned through chattering teeth.

Lucy tugged against her leash in the direction of home. I let her pull me back toward the house, but our path was blocked as we turned the last corner to safety.

"What the—" was all I got out. This *thing* held a hand up, but not in a wave. It was more like a threatening fist. Yes, *thing. It* wasn't human.

Lucy snarled and tried to lunge at it, but my tight grip held her. The size difference would have prevented her from winning. It stood about seven feet and was covered with brown fur. I blinked, hoping it was a bear standing up. It wasn't. It was Bigfoot.

"Come on, Lucy." I yanked her leash, and we ran in the opposite direction.

Its footsteps thundered behind us. I didn't know where I could run to, just that I needed to keep going or we wouldn't survive this encounter. Rain pelted us like angry bees as we raced along the path. I slipped but didn't fall.

The sounds stopped. Maybe we'd lost the thing—I refused to waste time looking. I ran on. My heart rammed into my ribs, and each breath was shallower than the last. As I veered off the trail and cut through the woods back to the house, I knew my body wouldn't let me keep this pace up for much longer.

Once I got home, I could call for help. They wouldn't believe me, though. A better plan was to get into my car with Lucy and drive. Go anywhere but here. Leave the house. Rent it and buy another. I had enough money to do that. If only I had my keys with me. But I didn't, I'd have to go into the house and waste time. This wasn't looking good for us.

Pain stabbed through my side, but I kept going. I splashed through puddles. The sky lit up in streaks as the ground shook. The rain changed to hail, pelting down hard on us. As I stumbled over a tree root, I couldn't tell if anything was following.

"Great." I watched the ground coming toward my face, but a hand grabbed my clothes and pulled me upright before I hit.

"Be careful." The gentle voice came from a tall, muscular man, not Bigfoot.

"I—I was trying to get home in the storm and thought I saw something." I tried to catch my breath.

"Yes, I'm sure you saw that bear I ran across a ways back. I was hoping to run into someone. My car broke down." He had the most beautiful brown eyes, and wavy, dark hair framed his powerful jaw. He looked like a male model.

"You? Oh, yes, I can call you a tow if you like. My name is—"

He cut in, holding up a manicured hand before I could finish. "Yes, that's great. Call. I'm right up the road on the left side. I think you'd better get back to your house. You don't want to get hit by lightning or something else. I'll wait in my car."

I glanced at my house, wondering if going back there was even a good idea now. "Yes, well, um . . . okay."

He smiled. "You go on and make that call. If I see that bear again, I'll shoo it off and make sure it doesn't bother you again."

"What kind of car should I tell them you drive? We have a local—"

There was a grunt behind me. I spun around to see Bigfoot and a man I didn't recognize in what looked like a wrestling match to the death. The man's eyes were dark as night, as the two clashed with punches that landed with deadly precision. They were evenly matched.

"Go!" Bigfoot yelled in the gentle voice of the man I had just spoken with.

Lucy pulled away and lunged at them. Bigfoot grabbed her by the collar and tossed her to the side. She landed on her back with an *oomph*.

"Lucy!" I cried, racing to her side. I wouldn't leave her behind.

A loud, piercing scream overshadowed the storm.

"Come on, girl," I encouraged. She pulled herself up and nudged me with her nose. "You're okay!"

The loud grunts of the fighting continued. Bigfoot appeared to be losing ground against the nimble man. I had stepped into one of my stories. Or had the stories always been there? Maybe I wasn't such a talented writer.

"Go!" The Bigfoot creature roared.

"Yes, please go." The other man, dressed all in black that matched his mesmerizing night eyes, had a voice like a bass guitar. I swear I saw a dark outline of wings, but I blinked and they were gone. "Bigfoot and I have a playdate."

I didn't need any encouragement. Lucy and I ran. The glow of the porch light illuminated the path to my house. I raced up the deck stairs when something grabbed my arm. I turned, wide-eyed, to face the mythical creature that I didn't believe in.

"They found you!" he roared. "We told you to keep a low profile."

"What the hell are you talking about?" I yelled as the furry creature turned back into the man I had spoken to about a broken-down car.

His eyes softened, and he put a gentle hand on my shoulder. "I knew you had stayed too long in human form, Sena. No one believed me when I said you'd forget. You can't stay here anymore. They've located you. You are marked."

I pushed down the feeling of trust I got from his sparkling eyes. *Trust no one.* "I think you have some issues. I'll call you a tow, but you'd better leave."

He shook his head. "You're one of us, remember? Come on, you know. Think. You can be like I am. Remember me? I'm Tarwin."

I shook my head. "No. I don't know what you're talking about."

"No time for this. Sorry, Sena." He wrapped a strong, warm hand around my neck, and everything went black.

I woke up in bed. It was soft and safe, like a cocoon. Lucy was by my side. *It was a dream.* I stretched and smiled, but my contentment disappeared as a tall, upright reptile entered the room.

"It's time to go home, Sena. I can help you out of your skin." It was Tarwin's voice. He looked exactly the way they portrayed aliens in movies: green, scaly skin, huge black eyes, and a long, thin head. I blinked, and he was Bigfoot again. This was crazy. He had to be a shapeshifter. Behind him was the man with night eyes, who did have wings but not the angelic kind.

"Look out!" I cried, jumping out of bed.

"Still doing your alien act to get their skin, Tarwin?" The man with dark eyes grinned.

"Look out, Sena. He's a monster!" Tarwin circled the man.

The man shook his head. "You should go now, Sena, while I do my job and rid the world of another evil shapeshifter."

Matching the speed of the other man, Tarwin as Bigfoot whirled, holding a gun. My gun. They fought over it. The gun went off, making a large hole in my wall. Blood coated the blue flowered wallpaper. I didn't wait for the outcome. Instead, I grabbed Lucy and raced out of the room, leaving them behind. I snatched my car keys from the hook in the kitchen, grabbed my purse from the table, and slipped into my clogs. A gleam caught my eye as I turned. My knives had been laid out neatly on the kitchen table with plastic under them.

A serial killer would do that, not an alien trying to help me. I gulped and raced to my car, starting it with the fancy button on my fob that I never thought I'd use. The engine turned over before I even got in. Lucy jumped onto the passenger seat, and I slammed the door. We skidded into a right turn to get out of the driveway.

I chanced one glance back. The man with the night eyes smiled and waved, then he disappeared into the forest right as my house burst into flames. I turned onto the road and didn't stop driving until I was safely in town.

I will never forget what really happened that day, but I stuck to the best story: I had escaped a serial killer. Weeks later, the police report backed it up officially.

The young officer peered over the report. "Larry Kemp. We've been looking for him for a long time. Too bad he set your house on fire, but at least we located his remains. He won't be hurting anyone else. You were fortunate to have escaped him."

No mention of Bigfoot or shapeshifters or men with wings. Frankly, I didn't care. I pushed the images out of my mind.

I bought a house by the ocean and continued writing with Lucy by my side. I avoided any mention of knives or shapeshifters. That would make it too real. The menacing presence was gone, but the man with the night eyes and dark wings appeared occasionally. He'd smile and wave to me. I felt no fear with him there. I guess he turned out to be the good guy.

Finally I found my peace and sanity next to the gentle Pacific waves. The man with the night eyes had to be my muse and protector. Which made me safe, didn't it?

The Dolphin

For James, Kahlan, Aurora, and Kyla

THE COOL WINTER sun reflected off the blue ocean, making my eyes water. I blinked hard to clear my vision as I dove back in. Why did my children and grandchildren huddle on the white, sandy beach? Didn't they want to swim with me? My oldest grandson, Peter, walked to the water's edge. He tossed a lei of pink plumeria into the waves. Those flowers reminded me of the beautiful day Bob and I renewed our vows for our fiftieth wedding anniversary on a stunning Hawaiian beach.

I jumped high into the air and called out, "Where did you get the flowers, Peter?"

An enormous wave crashed against the rocks, drowning out my words.

Peter stood with his arms folded over a black shirt and the dolphin tie I'd bought him when he graduated from college last year. The incoming waves soaked the bottom of his black pants.

I shook my head and tried again. "The water's great! Join me!"

Louder breaking waves masked my words, leaving only a whistle.

A small pod of dolphins approached and swam urgently around me.

"What's wrong? Are you protecting me?" I scanned the area, but there were no sharks or other dangers.

A lone dolphin seemed to be watching me. A familiar chill ran through me as another gently brushed against my legs. I dove underwater to get a better look.

Was it? *No.* I shook my head. It was a silly fantasy to believe my beloved husband would return as my favorite mammal. Although the dolphin held my stare, it was just curiosity. I shook my head and kicked to the surface, only to find my family leaving.

"Hey! Where are you going?" But only a high-pitched noise that the waves didn't hide came from my lips. I'd lost my voice.

Peter was the only one left standing on the edge of the ocean. He met my gaze, smiled, and pointed to his tie. Then he wiped the tears off his face and put on black-framed sunglasses. What he did next tugged heavily on my heart. My sweet grandson blew me a kiss, just like he had as a small boy when it was time to leave Grandma and Grandpa's house.

"Peter!" I yelled, yet nothing but that strange sound came out.

He paused and offered a wave before picking up his black shoes. He soon disappeared with everyone else I loved.

The lei was floating in a patch of gray powder that reminded me of when we scattered Bob's ashes into the ocean last year. I swam to the flowers and found a paper card attached.

Mother and Grandmother, you will be missed and forever loved.

I couldn't catch my breath. It all came crashing back to me with the force of a spring-loaded trap. I was in an uncomfortable hospital bed, suffering through too many tests. I never had peace with the forever beeping machines.

In my drugged haze, my doctor's sad tone gave me the needed

answer. "There's nothing else we can do except make her comfortable."

The cancer battle was over, and I was ready to let go. There was that moment when I hovered over my withered body, grateful to be free of the pain. Then there was a bright light, and I ended up here.

I grinned. It had happened! I turned in a circle, and a dolphin's tail, not my legs, greeted me.

The same dolphin was staring at me. It whistled and clicked until the high-pitched sounds became words I could understand. "Darci! I've been waiting for you!"

"Bob! I can't believe it. I've missed you so much."

"I've missed you too, sweetheart."

We'd found each other again. Words couldn't come fast enough as we caught up. We swam comfortably in our blessing long after Bob's pod had moved on.

It was just the two of us, and we happily explored the new world. We avoided humans, killer whales, and sharks, or maybe they avoided us. We were never sure, but time passed in the same blur as our human lives had.

One day, a lone dolphin swam up when we were peacefully investigating the purple, pink, red, green, and blue that mingled in the coral reefs off the Big Island in Hawaii. The eyes were so familiar that I immediately knew it was Peter.

Our joy at that moment could only be expressed in high, spinning jumps. After the celebration, we quickly caught up and learned that our grandson had been a famous author, raised three boys, and had a happy marriage.

"You kept your promise, Grandma. You said you'd come back as a dolphin when you left me. I knew that was you when we scattered your ashes."

"Yes, it was me. Grandpa was there waiting for me."

Peter blew out some bubbles. "They scattered my ashes in Hawaii, where Lacy and I married forty years ago. It was cancer like you, Grandma." He turned away. "I'll be right back. I'm going to say goodbye."

As the years passed, our pod grew as our family slowly joined us, including ones we'd never met in life, like Peter's fantastic wife and children. To this day, our family still explores the ocean. With our high leaps, we offer gratitude for the special gift we've been given. Maybe you've seen us and felt our joy?

Lyrical Dragon

THE WALK home from the general store was hot and dusty on the red dirt road. Sweat poured down Janie's face as she labored to carry the burlap sack of provisions her uncles had sent her to get. Because of their poor farming skills, almost everything had to be bought, and what extra money they'd had in the past disappeared when her mother did. Her uncles wouldn't comment on where her mother had gone, but Janie had her suspicions. The town's rumor mill, overheard on one of her shopping trips, decided her mother had run off with a man. Janie knew her mother wouldn't leave her only child behind with these lazy, no-good men.

"They will pay for whatever they did to my mother. I promise you that, Lyrical Dragon."

Heat radiated from the tiny green dragon charm that bounced against what Uncle Barry called her flat boy chest. The necklace was the only thing Janie had left from her mother, so she hid it well around her greedy relatives. They'd sell anything of value so they didn't have to work. With her mother gone, she was the only one left to provide food. The rains had stopped, and the garden was withering in the scorching sun. Water was limited, and everything was fading away except her fat uncles.

Janie's stomach growled from constant hunger. This chicken dinner wouldn't be for her. Instead, she was *allowed* to eat what she could find, which came down to a tiny fish from the dwindling creek or a rabbit—if she could catch one. At least they still had a milk cow and three laying hens. Before her uncles arose, Janie would squirt warm milk into her mouth before filling the bucket and hide an egg she could cook after they went out drinking and gambling. She had grown numb to the sweet smell of pancakes, bacon, and eggs every morning. They'd throw a pancake or piece of bacon at her for amusement if she was lucky. But as their meals got smaller, that little game stopped.

The only thing that still thrived on the grimy farm was an old apple tree that Janie watered daily. Harvest time was soon, and she planned to can the apples like Mother used to do before the fight with her uncles. She wished she knew what the argument had been about. All she'd overheard was her uncles telling her mother she'd have to deal with it. Her mother's response was *no more*. When Janie got back, her mother was gone.

As soon as Janie stepped inside the tiny cabin, she was hit with the odors of liquor, tobacco, and sweat. She shuddered and got to cooking. She prepared, served, and cleaned up the meals as her mother had done. Her mother had been a servant to them, and she was replaced with Janie, except now there were consequences. If the food wasn't hot enough, she would get a beating. If she didn't serve them fast enough, or if she broke a dish, another beating. She learned on the first day to be quiet and efficient and not ask questions. Her uncles never used to raise a hand to her until her mother vanished, but those days were gone.

The uncles had cleared out the room she and her mother used to share. They sold the bed and dressers and all her mother's clothes.

"You belong with the ugly animals." Uncle Barry had roared with laughter and poked Uncle Harry's side with his elbow.

"Sure didn't get her mother's looks, that's for sure. But she can cook, so there's no need to sell her yet." Uncle Harry let loose a long, loud burp and wiped his prickly face with the back of his greasy hand.

"Not yet. We may have promised Mother we'd care for our sister, but she didn't say anything about her brat. Wait till she sprouts some pillows on the front. Someone will pay good money for her." Uncle Barry pushed back his oily red hair. "What are you looking at, girl? Want a beating?"

Janie knew she'd better get out of their sight and raced out of the house, chased by their laughter.

That first night in the barn, she settled into a pile of hay with a brown horse blanket that had belonged to the horse they'd sold. The last horse stood quietly in her stall, as if she knew she was next. Her uncles rode tandem on the thin brown mare on their nightly ride into the saloon.

Today in the store, Janie had been pelted with evil gossip from the preacher's wife and another woman she didn't recognize.

"I hear those no-good Power brothers owe Jake Mallon over five hundred dollars from gambling. That whole family is trash. Why, even the girl's mother—" The plump, red-headed preacher's wife had the grace to stop talking when she spotted Janie. The other woman rolled her beady brown eyes, narrowed her gaze into a sneer, and smoothed down her crisp gray skirt.

A flush crept across Janie's face as she counted the money, gathered her meager supplies, and raced out of the store.

"That is one odd child," commented the preacher's wife.

Janie raced through the small town without looking back. She wished her uncles' gambling and debts weren't her concern, but flat-chested or not, she'd end up as the payment when Jake Mallon or whoever else they owed came collecting.

She blew out the oil lamp and pulled the little green-and-gold necklace her mother had playfully called the Lyrical Dragon from under her bodice. She gave it a gentle kiss.

"Soon I'll belong to someone else. Maybe they'll be better to me."

The full moon shone through the barn's cracks. One beam hit the forest-green glass of the dragon and lit up its red eyes like a bonfire. The necklace's heat intensified so much that it burned her fingers.

Janie dropped it. "Ouch! Maybe it held my body heat or something." She blew on her throbbing fingertips.

The chickens let out a quiet cluck, and the cow, whom her mom had named Tansey, mooed softly.

"Goodnight. Sleep tight, Tansey." Janie patted the hay, searching for her necklace, and quickly located it. She laid it next to her. "I'll put you on in the morning, Lyrical Dragon."

She burrowed down into her prickly bed and closed her eyes as she heard her uncle's laughter coming from the house. They hadn't left for town yet. That wasn't a good sign.

A small voice drifted up from the hay.

I am by your hand
please put me back on your neck
your time here is short

Janie's heart took off like a rabbit running from a mountain lion. She sat up and picked up the stick she had used to prop the door open. "Who's there? I have a gun and know how to use it." She tried to merge into the shadows, holding her fake stick gun.

The voice sounded like it was singing. It called out again.

full of bright magic,
I'm your lyrical dragon
we must return home

Janie's mouth went as dry as the barren soil. A moonbeam found the necklace. She carefully picked up the dragon, shaking like a leaf on the apple tree in a windstorm. Its red eyes glowed, but it wasn't hot anymore. "You can speak?"

when needed, I speak
bad men buried your mother...
by the apple tree

Janie almost dropped the Lyrical Dragon again. It pulsated in her hand like a heartbeat. She gasped. "Bad men? Do you mean my uncles killed my mother?"

your mother can't rule
killer brothers won't govern
you are meant to lead

Tears filled Janie's eyes, and then she let all her pain escape as she curled up in a ball, sobbing silently into her hands. Finally she was left with nothing but questions. She sat up and brushed the hay off her mended black skirt.

"Lyrical Dragon, my mother gave you to me right before she . . . " She couldn't say it out loud yet. "Mother told me my necklace would keep me safe, but she didn't mention you could talk—or say anything about leading. Why do you talk so oddly?"

my words lyrical.
I was with you, not Cassie
it's you that I save

Janie gulped loudly and cleared her throat. She spoke in a soft tone. "She knew she was going to die, didn't she?"

The Lyrical Dragon blinked its red eyes but didn't respond.

"My mom taught me to read and write when my uncles weren't around. She used to make up magical poems for me about our life here and called them haiku-like. She said she couldn't put nature in her words like a haiku required because it was so ugly here. Your words sound like those poems. I remember they had a pattern of syllables: five, seven, and five. That's what you sound like to me."

A moonbeam enveloped the Lyrical Dragon and lit him up like a lantern. He nodded but still didn't speak.

"She often described a beautiful place where waterfalls flowed into clear, sweet pools of water. She said she was happy there, but the war came, and she and her brothers found safety here. But those were just her stories. I don't believe that place exists, but her haikus about it were awfully pretty."

The dragon's red eyes softly glowed like an autumn-toned sunset.

it's where you belong
I'm real there, and you'll rule
the war is over

"Will my uncles return with us?" Janie twisted a lock of her golden hair around her fingers.

a killer's karma
they die painfully tonight
your kingdom awaits

Janie jumped up and looked around. "Are we safe?"
The dragon nodded.
"What about my mom's grave and the animals? They need tending to."
He shook his green head.

bodies mean nothing
her sweet soul protects you now
your grandma lingers

Janie shook her head and pinched her arm. "This has to be a dream, pain or not. My grandma? There was only my mother and her horrible brothers." She slapped her face, but nothing changed.

The Lyrical Dragon blinked and held her gaze.

Several horses clopped into their yard. An unfamiliar male voice boomed. "Let's burn them out and have some fun!"

"No need for a fire! Kill them!" a harsh voice responded.

There were two loud thumps and whimpers. She was positive her cowardly uncles were trying to run away.

The voice was still bellowing. "There they are—get them!"

"Don't hurt us. Take the girl, cow, and chickens, Jake." Uncle Harry's voice was whiny, like a small child's.

There was a slight laugh that held no warmth in it. "I plan to do both. First, the horses want to show you what a ground ride is. Although your skin might not like it when we drag you to town."

"No, please!" Uncle Barry screamed.

Harsh laughter was the only response.

The Lyrical Dragon's glow stroked her hands, sending a sweet peace.

belong on your neck.
close your eyes, my sweet princess
my magic returns

Janie didn't want these men to find her, so what did she have to lose? She slipped the dragon necklace over her head and closed her eyes tightly. A surge rushed through her body, like being startled by a nasty rattlesnake. That feeling was more potent than her uncles' cruel words or blows.

The stale air of the barn and the prickly hay evaporated, and in their place was a sweet scent that reminded her of fresh apples on a warm day and the flowers they used to have. The only flowers that had survived the drought were yellow daisies, but those had died out last season. There was a pleasant sound of water flowing over rocks. A cool, wet breeze caressed her skin, and grass tickled her legs. Janie was afraid to open her eyes, so she reached for the Lyrical Dragon. He was gone.

"You may open your eyes now. I'm over here, Princess Janine."

Janie slowly opened her eyes to a green dragon the size of a house. His scales were gold-trimmed, and his red eyes were now brown. His muscular legs had enormous claws on the end of them, and his long tail was barbed like a fence. He bent down to look at her and held her gaze. His smile was full of teeth. The most beautiful waterfall framed him.

She hopped up and took a quick step back from the massive creature. "Where am I?"

The dragon bowed his head. "Home."

Janie took in the lush green foliage around the pond the crystal-clear water flowed into. It was like her mother had described. Flowers of every size and color filled the tranquil scene. The bees' hum and the butterflies' grace seemed so normal in a completely abnormal situation. She shook her head as a heavy sense of foreboding gripped her.

She inched away from the imposing dragon toward the thick tree line. She thought he'd have difficulty following her in. "You aren't speaking in poetry anymore. How do I know it's you?"

The dragon let out a long breath and settled down on the forest floor like he was trying to make himself look smaller. He wasn't having much luck. "It's me. I took you away from that horrid place before those men captured you. The spell that changed me dissipated once the danger that made you and your mother flee from here was gone. I am back to myself, and you can call me Lyric."

Janie's shoulders relaxed. Was it some magic that was making her trust this thing? She was near the tree line. She could hide there and figure this out, if she could outrun a dragon who might breathe fire. "So, Lyric, we're back. What am I supposed to do now? I have no family."

He shook his broad head, breaking off a lower branch of the white flowering tree next to him. "No, Princess Janine, I don't think you do anymore. The queen's life force faded away. I'm sorry. She wanted to see you before she passed. The war ended when they captured and killed General Max a few hours ago. He was the one you and the rest of the family were hidden from. His potions killed your grandma, the queen. If you had stayed here, it would have been the same for you and the rest. His magic didn't work where you were."

"Why should I believe anything you're saying?" Janie tensed her body, ready to bolt.

"Princess, I don't want to chase you, but I will. It still isn't safe for you here yet. The people who follow him will come after you. Even without their powerful magic, they are still a danger to you. Take a deep breath and focus. You have it inside of you to know what I know. Try, please. Focus on your grandmother."

Janie stepped into the dark forest and stopped. What would it hurt to try? She was within the trees now. She breathed in the woodsy scent, and soothing energy radiated from the trees surrounding her. A small scarlet bird flew down and settled on the branch next to her. "Hello, little bird. I wish I knew what to do," she whispered.

The bird nodded and then flew down and settled on her shoulder. Janie smiled at it and reached up to stroke it. "I—"

Images came quickly, one after another. She was standing on a fancy chair, looking out a window. There was a bloody battle no one had wanted her to witness right outside the tall stone walls. Soldiers bravely fought for their kingdom and kept her and her family safe. In the middle of the gory fighting was a man with what looked like red eyes, long, black, stringy hair, and a black cloak. He held a long, wooden staff with a glowing red light. He extended his arm and pointed up at her. Heat coursed through her body as her mother yanked her away.

"We told you to stay away from the windows. It isn't safe."

The next thing she knew, a man with a red beard, dressed all in leather, entered the room, ready for battle with his bow and arrow. He bowed, whispered to her mother, and fastened a necklace around her neck. It had a small glass charm—the Lyrical Dragon. The man with the red beard bowed and left.

"It's time, sweetheart. Your daddy isn't coming home. Gather your things. We have to go."

A gray-haired, careworn woman wearing a silver crown sparkling with diamonds entered the room. Her green velvet dress flared out as she rushed to Janie's mother. Tears overflowed her blue eyes as they hugged.

Then she bent down and gathered Janie into her arms. "My angel. I will miss you, but I must stay here and fight for our kingdom. You'll be safe where you're going, and once it's secure, the Lyrical Dragon will bring you back home. You won't remember anything of your life or that he's a dragon. It's the only way you can stay safe. I love you and hope I can hold you again."

Janie's mother bowed her head and sighed. "I wish you were coming with us, Mother."

Her grandmother stood tall and adjusted her crown. "I can't. I am the queen. I must stay here and save our home. Go now, before his magic holds you here and fills you with evil. I am strong and can fight it, I promise you. Know I love you both and your brothers will watch over you until it's safe to return."

After a quick hug, everything blurred until they ended up in that dreary, dusty place where nothing was ever the same again.

The small red bird rubbed its head against Janie's cheek and brought her back to her current reality. It bowed its head. A soft message raced through her mind. "You will be queen someday and lead well. General Richards will keep our land safe until you're ready. You can trust him and Lyric. And sweetness, remember you are loved." It flew away.

"Now what am I supposed to do?" Janie waited for an answer that didn't come.

She shrugged her shoulders and peeked through the trees. The dragon had stayed in the same spot, waiting.

He spoke in a gentle tone. "You know?"

"Yes."

"You saw the bird?"

She nodded and slowly made her way to the dragon.

His eyes filled with tears. "The queen was strong. She saw you one more time. She helped you remember. I would feel better, Princess, if we left here. You will be safe in my cave, away from the kingdom. My mate is there waiting for us. We will not hurt you. You believe that, don't you?"

The small red bird flew over them; and with that, she felt a comforting calm. "I don't know why, but I trust you. This is all so confusing."

"I understand. We will have to fly there." He lowered himself so he was lying flat.

She hesitated only momentarily, then climbed aboard and settled on his back like he was a horse. The scales were soft against her legs. She grabbed the protruding fin on the back of his neck.

"Are you secure, Princess?"

"Yes, I think so."

"Hang on tight."

In a single jump, they were airborne. She slid, and her stomach rolled. The dragon adjusted so he was more level.

"Wedge your feet between my scales. It won't hurt me."

Her feet found warmth underneath. It stabilized her quickly. The air blew her hair, and she soon felt more freedom than she had riding the farm horses. She wondered what evil lurked in the dense forest. Would it come after her the way it had her uncles? No, she wasn't weak like them.

"Over there, that will be your home someday. However, you have much to learn first, Princess. My mate and I can teach you."

The trees cleared on their left, and a rose-colored palace jutted high above the tallest tree. Chunks were missing, like an enormous monster had tasted it.

"Home." She sighed.

It had taken a beating, as they all had, but at least it was where she belonged. Someday she would have to take her grandmother's place. She hoped she was strong enough for that crown.

This Journey

99 Words

WE'VE MADE this journey by horse every year on our wedding anniversary. The only stop was to admire the beauty of the sunset before setting up camp by the gently flowing creek. This was our place. I know you'll be there waiting for me. That's why I brought your horse. We'll ride as spontaneously as we did in youth, with the winds tangling our hair and the carefree laughter running freely. I won't leave you until you have to go, my love. Then I'll go home comforted, knowing that we can stay here for eternity when my time comes.

The Bench

IT WAS OUR BENCH. The pain of that familiar tug at my heart was always close by. I quickened my pace and maneuvered through the pungent orange, red, and yellow leaves, trying to outrun it. I hated making this walk alone through the fall splendor.

When something brushed against my leg, I jumped.

"Sorry. Lady escaped from her collar again."

The pug sat at my feet with an amiable head tilt. "No problem," I mumbled.

"She's friendly if you want to pet her."

I shook my head and stepped around the dog. I kept going past the brightly lit coffee shop that often provided me with a latte. Finally I plopped down on a cold concrete bench and was immediately greeted by a distant chorus of barking dogs.

A young boy burst through a door directly across the street. He was cradling a tiny black kitten.

"Can I name him Skitter, Mom?"

As the mother agreed, I returned to the day I brought my kitten home from this animal shelter. Felix died right before his eighteenth birthday. After crying for two weeks, I decided I didn't want to endure that heartbreak again.

A wind kicked up, and the sun was sloping down. It was time for me to head home. I pushed myself up from the bench but froze when a young couple exited the building with a small, exuberant black lab just like . . . Tears flowed unchecked down my face. I missed my walking companion, Bessie. I had to put her to sleep after she lost her battle with cancer, and it tore me apart, holding her for the last time. My two constant companions were taken from me in the space of two months. Now I was a widow and petless at sixty-five years old. With a heavy heart, I slowly made my way home.

A-hundred yards before turning into my driveway, I heard a muffled cry coming from a bush.

"Hello?" I called out, getting my keys ready to run inside.

It answered with a whimper.

"Pup?"

I carefully pushed the branches aside and found a taped cardboard box.

"Oh, God."

My heart was racing as I ripped the box open and peered inside. A yellow puppy barked and jumped on the side of the box with its tail wagging. I quickly scooped it up, and it nestled into my neck. The smaller black one wasn't moving, and the black-and-yellow puppy could barely lift its head.

"You poor babies! What kind of monster would do this?"

I raced to my car and gently set the box down, still hanging on to the yellow puppy. My hand brushed over the black pup, finding no life, but the other pup sighed as I stroked its soft fur.

My hands shook as I called the vet and started the car. "I found some puppies in terrible shape. Are you still open?"

"We just closed, but bring them in, Marsha. We'll wait."

Soon, the two puppies who had survived were on the vet's examination table.

"They're around four weeks old and look like a shepherd/lab

mix. It was lucky you found these two when you did. We'll do everything we can for them and call you in the morning. Are you considering keeping them?"

I frowned. "I don't think so, but I'll pay for whatever they need."

I spent a long night tossing and turning. Their sweet faces
haunted me, along with the cruelly taped box. I knew I was meant to
find them, but that didn't mean I had to keep them. When the sun
finally rose, I knew what I had to do.

The phone rang after breakfast. "Hi, Marsha. I'm sorry, the boy
didn't make it, but the girl did. We'll keep her here another night so
we can monitor her, and we found someone to foster her, so—"

I cut her off. "No, she has a home with me."

A year later, Molly was proudly wearing her new pink collar. She
yanked me toward our bench. We couldn't sit there because a neighbor's adolescent daughter had taken it over with a box of kittens, a
FREE sign taped to the side. Our walk was cut short when I locked
eyes with a tiny black cat. We had found the missing member of our
family, and I had learned that having a pet's love was worth enduring
any loss.

When The Lights Go Out

People will tell you that fiction is only make-believe. Don't let them fool you. Some of it is real. But maybe if you knew the truth, you'd never sleep again. Right now, I'm resting but hooked on monitors and medication, with a different perspective on life.

Sleep has been hard for a long time because fantasy has become a reality for me. Oddly, *they* have always been okay with me discussing *them* as fiction. I would have gone crazy if I hadn't written it down. *They* were so confident that no one would believe me. I think it amused *them* that my stories talked about the cliché things that go bump in the night.

What I'm about to tell you is not a fictional story. Whether or not you believe me, I can do nothing about it. I hope that those who have seen what I have will be comforted by my words.

Some of our darkest nightmares and things we imagine in the shadows are real. This knowledge prevented me from leaving my home at night. I stayed safely inside my brightly lit house. Could *they* get in? Of course, but it was the best I could do. Luckily, *they* preferred the darkness. I knew I was being watched whenever I fell asleep, even with all the lights on. Illumination only encouraged *them* to keep their distance. Still, I never understood what *they* were waiting for until that night. Before that moment, I figured *they* enjoyed the hunt or just liked observing.

Have you seen something from the corner of your eye and laughed it off? Or got that uncomfortable feeling of being watched in the middle of the night? As a kid, I tried to tell my parents what I saw. A knowing look always passed between my mother and father, and then they would assure me nothing was lurking under my bed, but I kept my feet safely away from the sides of the mattress.

This probably sounds like the rambling of a sick old woman, but I'm as sane as any of you. I can tell you what year it is and who's the president. I can also give you the capital of every state and country. Even in my groggy condition, I've thought about what would be said about me if I told this story. Best-selling horror author Bea Cant believes her own words.

Math was my major in school before I found my love of writing. So I tried to apply a logical formula to explain what was happening to me, with no luck. Last week, my power went out, and the generator didn't come on like it was supposed to. What a waste of $15,000 for a system that failed me when I needed it the most. And there I was, alone in the dark. Every sound was amplified in that silence.

I got a flashlight and lit every candle I owned. I prepared myself for the things that creep around without light. They were watching me, and I could feel it.

"I know you're there." My weak voice gave away my fear.

There was a slight giggle. These *things* didn't even have the courtesy to pretend. A quick flash from the corner of my eye was one thing, but finally hearing them caused my heart to do an uncomfortable flip.

"I'm done with you! I refuse to write about horror anymore. You aren't important, so go away." I pushed the words past my dry throat.

Another high-pitched giggle, closer this time. Light in that direction reflected off a pair of blood-red eyes.

My heart did another flip like it was jumping on a trampoline.

Was I headed for a heart attack? A loud thump echoed in the silence next to my bed. The light beam showed my pen and notebook on the hardwood floor. Piercing laughter that resembled a woman's drunken glee surrounded my space.

Breathlessly, I forced out my words. "What do you want?"

A deep growl responded.

I jumped back, hitting the back of my knees on the bed, which landed me sitting on my satin comforter. I tried to swallow, but my mouth was as dry as a drought-stricken pond.

That giggle came out of the darkness again, followed by a small child's voice. "Please, be calm. All we want you to do is write."

I took a long breath and reached for my bottle of water. It soothed my throat and settled my racing heart. "I will not write anymore. Move on. It's not like you have to worry about me. No one would believe the truth." I stroked the soft material. That usually calmed me after a bad dream, but the motion didn't ease a living nightmare.

"We know." More giggling. "We insist you write."

"If you know, then why insist? I'm done with horror."

"Horror writing opened you to us. We *insist* you write because you are our recorder. You tell our history for future generations."

I felt myself again after a few more sips of cool water. I eased up from the bed and put my hands on my hips. "Find someone else."

The red eyes blinked. "Other writers are useless to us because we can't channel our stories through them as we have with you. You live well because our words fill your thoughts. Try thinking of us as your muses, and we promise to avoid scaring you." The voice was closer, and those eyes glowed a bright ember red, but I still couldn't spot the creature.

"Scare away. I do not want to be a muse or record history for whatever you are."

The voice had a purr, much like if a tiger could speak. "Here on Earth, we are your nightmares, but on our planet, we just are."

I had thrown my extra blanket around my shoulders, but the chill this creature brought went deep into my bones. *Maybe if I left.*

"We'd follow you," responded the tiny voice. It could read my mind. "You'll feel safe when you're writing. You'll see, my pet."

I inched around the foot of the bed toward my purse. "I never feel safe."

"We haven't hurt you yet, have we?"

I shrugged. "No. Not physically but mentally. I feel crazy."

"You aren't crazy, just creative. You can't work in the dark tonight. Why don't you go to bed? I promise, you are safe."

"No." I fought the sudden exhaustion.

"This is all a dream." Its sweet voice soothed me.

I shook my head to stay awake and scooped up my cell phone. "This is *not* a dream. I want to see you. See what you are."

"Your heart. We worry about it, my pet."

"I'm not a pet. Show me." I tucked my phone safely into my pocket.

There was a sigh that sounded more like a dog's growl. "You want it your way."

"I do." I slipped my stocking feet into gray clogs and found my purse on the floor. Luckily I was still wearing the oversized sweatshirt and leggings that had become a uniform. I had all I needed to start over. My huge purse was more of a go-bag for fire season—I took nothing out. It had all my important papers, jewelry, a computer flash drive, and old photos. Everything else could be replaced.

"Put your purse down and go to bed. You are being silly, my p— Bea. You can't believe we will let you leave, can you?"

I yanked on my jacket and grabbed my keys. "What does it matter if I leave? Can't you follow me?"

No response to that. Maybe there was some hope. I opened the door and used my phone for light. I wasn't even going to lock it behind me or worry about the candles. What for? I wasn't coming back.

"Bea. Come back to us. We won't hurt you," the voice cooed.

With no response, I stepped into the frigid night and slammed the heavy wooden front door behind me. Armed only with the flashlight on my cell phone, I rushed into the darkness. I clicked my car door open, slid onto the leather seat, and shut the door. I breathed out a sigh of relief when I locked the doors. No giggles or voices. Maybe they couldn't follow me.

A thought passed through my mind. *They can only stay with me if I let them.*

"I hope so," I mumbled as the engine turned over.

I reversed the car, never taking my eyes off the front door. Once I got turned around, I dared a glance back. The front door was open and framing a pair of red eyes. A form materialized, darker than the night. It was at least seven feet tall, with large fangs that glistened—or maybe glowed. I wasn't sure in the dim moonlight. The thing was covered in wild, dark hair and had long arms and legs. It didn't have a nose as we do, but there were large lips around those teeth. It smiled as it beckoned to me. A heavy weight made it hard to breathe. I had seen it, and here was the promised heart attack. I closed my eyes tightly and breathed deeply.

"No. You aren't going to win."

The pressure loosened its grip. It was trying to scare me to death.

"Not this time." I punched the gas pedal and peeled out of the driveway without looking back again.

I reached over to turn on the music when someone cleared their throat.

"Pull over," a woman's voice said.

I glanced in the back, but only the empty seat was there. They could follow me. I pulled over.

"Thank you. I do not want you to get in an accident, Bea."

I didn't respond. *There's no escape.*

"No, you are wrong. They lived in your house with you. They were invited. That is the only way, after all. You invited us too."

"What are you talking about?" I choked out as I gripped the steering wheel. My chest tightened again, and I sucked in deep breaths between the waves of pain.

"Yes, good. Breathe deeply. It would be best if you got medical attention before it gets worse. I will stay with you. After a brief hospital stay, you should be okay and have many more years. *If* all goes well, so keep taking those breaths, dear."

I let out a long exhale, and some of the pressure subsided. "I won't write for you."

"Oh, no, *we* are not like that. You can write, or not write, whatever you want. However, you may invite them back with your darker subjects. You were born with no natural protection against them."

I squinted. There was nothing but black leather and seatbelts. "So you're saying—oh, never mind. I must be completely crazy. Show yourself."

"No, I never do that. Sorry. I am not a monster. Most think we are beautiful. I never talk to humans, but I made an exception in your case. I held those monsters back long enough for you to escape. That is all you need to know."

I rubbed my shoulders and then rolled them to release the pain. "How did I invite them to me?"

"They were there when you were little. Your mom was . . . well, you know. She played with things she should not have. Opened a door with her Ouija board. Then those creatures stayed. They hung onto your talent, your lack of natural protection from them, and crept into your scary stories, which invited them. You stayed in your childhood house with them. We were there too, but you never found us. We tried to protect you, but you did not make it easy. You cannot go back there. We would never get you out again—alive, that is."

I shook my head and ran my fingers through my short, gray hair. My chest was loosening up, thankfully. "How do I know you aren't one of them?"

"Good question. They have red eyes, right?"

"Yes." I nodded and adjusted my seat belt, which was too tight on my left shoulder.

"Then I will show you my eyes. Will that work?"

"I think so."

Behind me appeared gentle green eyes. They were like a bright spring day, framed with heavy black lashes and topped with an arched brown eyebrow on creamy, tan skin. I let out my held breath. Nothing else appeared. "How do I know any of this is real? That those monsters can't change their eye color?"

"Would seeing my wings help?"

My hands tightened on the steering wheel. "Your wings? You're an angel?"

"Yes, that is what you call us."

The bluest wings opened up in the car. Why not show herself? This was crazy.

I gulped and faced the road. "Well, you have green eyes and blue wings, but still . . . "

"Still what, Bea? Oh, dear. It would be best if you got to the hospital. Things are speeding up. Drive, please."

I threw the car into gear. "I thought you said I had time."

The wings and eyes disappeared. "You did. Things change. Drive."

I pulled back onto the road and headed toward the hospital without further comment. My chest tightened, and it was getting hard to catch my breath.

Within minutes I pulled into the parking lot in front of the ER. "What is your name?" I asked as the pain increased.

"Andrea. Now please hurry, or you will not leave your car alive. I will talk to you more after the surgery. *Go!*"

I grabbed my purse, jumped out of the red Honda, and locked it. In a sweat, I tossed my keys into my purse and grabbed my medical card as I hurried through the hospital doors. The room spun as the security guard grabbed my arm.

"Are you okay, ma'am?"

"No, it's my heart. Help me." Then everything went black.

The next thing I remember is waking up in a hospital bed with monitors beeping next to me. I could barely open my eyes to see the nurse tending me.

"Oh, good, you're awake. Any pain?"

I shook my head.

A young redhead with a face full of freckles, she smiled brightly. "You made it here just in time. The doctor will be here to talk to you soon. You're going to be fine." She nodded and hurried out of the room.

"I have been here the whole time, Bea."

I peered into the dark room. "I can't see you. Who's here?"

"Andrea. Remember?"

I took a long, deep breath. "I thought . . . oh, never mind."

"I understand. Not to give you bad news immediately, but your house burned down. Those creatures left, now that the house is gone. I suggest you lighten up your writing so they do not return. Of course, that is up to you. I cannot keep talking to you—I should not even be telling you this much. But I want you to know that I will be here, and you are not alone. You should be able to feel that. Keep writing. You are important to this world."

Then Andrea showed herself. She was beautiful, like I imagined. Her long, flowing, platinum hair and mesmerizing golden gown, those azure wings . . . I wanted to write about them. Maybe I would.

"It is unlikely you will remember any of this, but maybe you will want to write about us. Who knows? Rest now, and I will stay here with you."

My eyelids grew heavy. "Thank you, Andrea."

She broke into a smile that lit up the room. "You are very welcome. It is time to heal."

A pair of red eyes appeared in the corner before I closed my eyes. I weakly pointed.

"Oh, dear. Another one. I *strongly* encourage you not to write about them anymore. You will be fine. They cannot hang around for long unless they are invited. Sleep." Andrea soothed me as I closed my eyes.

The red-eyed creature had that same childlike voice. "I can wait."

"So can I," Andrea replied.

I slowly opened my heavy eyelids. The furry monster grinned, showing teeth that glowed. "She's like her mother. She will invite us into wherever she makes a home."

"No, she is not. You will see." Andrea replied.

"Yes, we will."

I had almost drifted into sleep in the tense silence between monster and angel when the doctor entered the room rustling some papers. An older man with salt-and-pepper hair that curled around his ears, he seemed utterly unaware that the two beings watched his every move.

He put a warm, gentle hand on my arm. "Glad to see you are awake, Ms. Cant. I'm Dr. Howard. I will look after you during your stay here."

"I'm feeling groggy, Dr. Howard."

He nodded as he checked my pulse and vital signs. "To be expected after a major heart attack, but you arrived in time. The bypass was a success, and there was amazingly little damage. You're going to be fine. Just fine."

"Thank you."

He must have been over six feet tall but seemed smaller with a monster looming over him. "You are most welcome. I want to monitor you some more, but we'll have you back on your feet soon."

My focus shifted away from the otherworldly beings in the room. "I look forward to that and can't wait to get back to writing. I have a new book idea about a woman who solves murders with the help of an angel."

He wrote something on his paper and clamped the folder shut. "That sounds like a fine idea. But for now, no writing. Rest, and try not to move around too much for the next few hours."

I smoothed the beige blanket with the arm that didn't have an IV. "I can wait—and no more horror for me."

His blue eyes twinkled like his soul. Or perhaps that was the pain meds they had me on. A smile broke across his thin face. "I'm not a horror fan, but I know you're famous for that. I look forward to your new stuff."

"Thanks, Dr. Howard."

"You're welcome, Ms. Cant. I'll check back with you later. Rest." He shut the door behind him.

Andrea smiled smugly at the frowning monster. It shrugged and then left. "You are going to be okay. It is gone."

"Thank you." I closed my heavy eyes and listened to the comforting monitors. The nurse returned to take my vitals, but I pretended to be asleep. When she was gone, I opened my eyes to a room that only contained me, no angels or monsters. This is where I started this story, thanks to a notepad and pen left next to my bed. I hope someone believes me about the angel and that *thing*. Good won this time, or that was what I wanted to believe. I slept soundly for the first time in years.

In That Moment

IT WAS like every other evening when I slid into bed after my shower. The night was silent as I settled onto the cool, blue-flowered sheets. A dull thump of a headache pulsed behind my eyes as I checked the cell phone for messages, but I didn't find any. People were abuzz about strange lights in the sky on a local social media website. Giant glowing orbs were moving together in an unusually straight line. The official explanation was that it was a new group of satellites, but they didn't say who launched them. Some people online didn't buy that, and others had their theories. Ideas went from alien attack to secret government experiment. None of it sounded plausible, and I was too tired to pull myself out of bed to look.

My bed jolted like my husband, Sam, had bumped into the bed, but he wasn't home and I hadn't moved. This was when the talk changed from strange lights to earthquakes.

A text from my daughter, Tammy, popped up. *I got woken up by someone pounding on my front door. They were trying to get in. I can't get a response to my 9-1-1 call.*

I quickly responded. *I don't think anyone is trying to break in, but don't open the door to be safe. There has been a cluster of earthquakes, and I bet everyone calls it in.*

I sent her a screenshot from the app that monitors them while I quickly responded to three texts from friends asking if I was okay after the quakes and strange lights.

I'm fine. Like being back in the Bay Area! Ha!

Rarely did I feel the Earth move in my house in the mountains. I was no longer tired. With a sigh, I tugged on my gray bathrobe as my orange tabby, Leo, popped from under the bed.

"A cup of chamomile tea sounds good." Leo jumped up and settled onto my pillow. "I'll be needing that pillow later."

Leo held my gaze with his golden eyes as if to decide whether my wishes mattered. Coming to his usual cat decision to ignore me, he shut his eyes. I rubbed my temples as the headache's pressure increased and headed to the kitchen. Mother Nature's grumbling had dashed my plan to go to bed early. I filled the electric kettle with filtered water and switched on the TV to check if that promised big earthquake had finally happened. A message appeared on the screen informing me there was no signal from the satellite dish.

Right as the kettle beeped to let me know the water was hot, the lights went out.

"You're kidding me."

Luckily I had my cell phone. I turned on the flashlight, poured the hot water into my favorite blue mug, and added a tea bag. Without power, there was no internet, which meant I couldn't get any more news on my cell phone either. Sam had insisted we get a generator to run our fridge and well if this happened. I knew the loud machine was full of fuel, and three cans of gas would last me for days, or until he returned. It was an option, but I didn't feel like starting it. Besides, I was sure the power would come back at any moment.

A quick check of our landline revealed a chilling silence. What a time for the power *and* usually reliable landline to go out—while my husband and son-in-law were two hours away fishing. If Sam experienced the quake, he'd be worried about me home alone with Leo and our old lab mix, Francie, who had slept through all the excitement. There was no way to let him know we were okay—or to find out if he was.

"No more instant information for me tonight, Francie."

She opened her brown eyes and sighed, then got up with a grunt from her comfy bed and stood protectively next to my legs. I stroked her brown fur and grabbed my tea. I maneuvered down the dark hall with the light from my cell phone, Francie at my heels. Her face dropped as I shut the bathroom door, leaving her on the other side of it. I conserved the water, knowing we only had so much in our holding tank until I ran the generator, and used hand wipes instead of soap. When I opened the bathroom door, my protective dog was waiting.

I patted her head. "I know, girl. This is a crazy evening, with the lights and the ground shaking."

Francie settled down on the throw rug by the bed, sighed, and closed her eyes. I was glad for her company. As usual, I grabbed my e-reader to wind down before sleep, but I stared at the same page and couldn't focus on the words. I checked my phone, hoping a text might make it through, but there was nothing. At that moment, for all I knew, I could be the only person left alive on our planet. I finished my lukewarm tea and fluffed my pillow, which was now cat-free. The bed seemed so big tonight without my husband of thirty-five years snoring next to me. Arranging his pillows to fill up the space, I flipped on my belly and fell into a deep sleep without another thought to all the strangeness of the night.

Morning arrived with the powerless silence being filled by distant generators. As my bones crackled their greeting, I stretched, slowly rose, and slipped into my blue bear slippers and bathrobe. There would be no cooking on my electric stove, but I could start the generator to use the microwave and run the fridge. I checked my landline and found it was still dead and there was no way to get any news.

The one thing I could control was doing my usual morning

chores with the animals. Francie was already at the door. She did her business on the lawn and sprinted back to the door.

"No exploring today?"

She pushed past me and settled onto her bed.

"Okay, then, how about a treat?"

That got a mild tail wag.

"You must miss Daddy. So do I, but he'll be home tomorrow."

After cleaning Leo's cat box and feeding both my pets, I grabbed a handful of almonds and washed them down with a bottle of water. Wrangling my hair into submission and brushing my teeth, I threw on my favorite lazy day outfit, or what could have been PJs but wasn't.

"Time to start the generator," I told Francie, who was observing me. She uttered a loud exhalation and followed me to the garage.

"Well, here goes nothing."

I yanked on the hanging rope that released our garage door. I always worried I'd break it, but finally I was gifted with a *thump*. The garage door was heavy, but I pushed it open. Once I got that done, I rolled out the generator and followed the detailed list of instructions my husband had left for me. Soon the engine rumbled, and the garage lights came on.

"Success!" Francie wagged her tail in what had to be approval.

Since Sam was always here, I avoided starting the generator. This was a sweet victory. I strolled away from the noise and ended up at the end of our tree-lined driveway.

"I'll take you on a walk later and check on the Simpsons. Being in their eighties, they may need my expertise with their generator, but it wouldn't surprise me if they were up to date on the news. He has a ham radio." Francie sat at my feet, making it seem like I wasn't talking to myself. While we were standing there, not one car drove by.

"Nobody out today. Guess because it's Saturday."

Francie's eyes never strayed from me.

"Ready to go back inside? I'm excited about my morning tea." She raced to the garage at an impressive speed considering her age. I took one more look down the road. The emptiness gave me chills.

After I drank my Earl Gray, I got to work. I ran a long extension cord through the house and plugged in our internet. I watched the green and red lights blinking as they turned on. Then a bright red light stayed on, telling me *No, you can't have what you want.*

"So that's down too. Great." Right then, a siren rushed past our house. At least someone was out today. I tugged on my gray sweater.

"Come on, Francie. Let's go check on the Simpsons." I clipped on her new pink cow-themed leash, and we were in the driveway when the familiar blue truck pulled in, minus the boat.

Sam slammed on his brakes and shut off the truck. His face was red, his hair wild like he hadn't slept.

"You're home early, Sam. Did you catch your limit already? And where—"

Sam held up his hands. "I'm so relieved you're okay, Nora. Don't you know what's going on?"

He pulled me into a tight hug. I held on to him, feeling safe for the first time since last night. "Going on?" The almonds and tea were at the back of my throat.

He pulled back and held my gaze. "We're at war. We need to make our way north. We're welcome there, but not here."

"War?"

"It finally happened. We're in a civil war, and the fighting is coming. We have to go where it's safe, further north."

"Leave our home? What about the kids?" My knees buckled, and Sam held me up.

"I'll be forced to fight for the rebels if we stay. I can't, and they'll kill anyone who won't join them."

"I'm sure the army will take care of them." I allowed myself to be led into the house.

"The army is gone. Those who were loyal were killed by those who weren't."

"How do you know this?" I pulled away and put my hands on my hips.

"I wasn't fishing. I was at a meeting. Those lights in the sky and what everyone thought were earthquakes were our last stand. Sweetheart, there isn't much time to explain. Tammy and Luke will be here soon with their trailer. We'll load up my pickup with provisions and head north."

"Was Luke with you?"

"Yes. He's getting Tammy."

"And David?"

His face reddened. "Our son is one of them now. He won't help us, and we can't help him."

My shoulders tensed. "Are you sure?"

"Yes, he let me pass the roadblock to get home because I was his father but warned me it would be the last time he would help a traitor." Sam's eyes filled with tears that he quickly wiped away.

I shook my head. "This can't be real."

Sam put his arm around me. I was a small, scared child at that moment. "But it is. You have a half hour to get what you think we need for colder weather. I'll bring the generator, tools, and weapons. It'll be okay, sweetheart, and our daughter and son-in-law will be with us. You know my cousins are up north, only eight hours away. We can stay with them."

I studied his expression, knowing he wasn't telling me everything. "We won't be coming back here, will we?"

He sighed loudly. "Plan for that, but hope for the best. Now go."

"I was going to check on the Simpsons. Shouldn't we warn them?"

"They're gone. I checked on the way home."

Soon we were following our daughter and son-in-law in a truck loaded with our irreplaceable belongings, like wedding and baby albums, jewelry, and important papers. The things we needed to survive included a tent, a power supply, canned food, clothing, water, camping supplies, a rifle, a handgun, and a healthy supply of bullets.

Luke and Tammy were driving their brand-new RV, which slept six. The thing I thought they were so foolish to go into debt for would be where we lived. Luke assured us they'd packed it with enough food to last a few weeks.

Francie settled into my lap while Leo slept in the carrier. We were refugees in a world that had suddenly turned upside down. A loud boom shook the road, and a fire truck raced by us with only one person inside. Smoke filled the sky, and flames shot up from the landscape where our home used to be. I grabbed Sam's hand as we drove silently into our future, leaving all we knew behind.

The Boy

BELLA SNAPPED the picture right before the boy disappeared. Finally she had proof that he existed. He had been in the same place for the last two weeks, right where the school bus dropped her off by their private road. He wore jeans and a gray hoodie and carried a black backpack. Without glancing back or speaking, he'd vanish into a heavy fog.

She raced down the long driveway to show her mother the photo. Mother sat on the porch in the old wooden rocking chair, sipping iced tea. The hair stood on Bella's arms when Mother's bloodshot eyes fixed on her. "Why do you have my camera?" Her words slurred together like they were in a wind tunnel, but the leaves on the trees were still.

"I borrowed it to get a picture of the boy. I got it. Look!" She held the camera up, hoping she was wrong about Mother's condition. The last three years had been peaceful now that she remained sober and took her meds.

Mother slammed the drink down hard, shattering the glass. "Liar! There's no boy out there, and stop calling me 'Mother.' You know I hate that word."

Bella sighed at the blood dripping from her mother's hand. That scary woman had returned. "Sorry, Stella. You're hurt. Where's Dad?" She scanned the area, hoping he had come home early.

"Gone. He was tired of raising another man's brat. I wish I'd never had you thirteen years ago." Stella sank into her chair and sobbed. Tears mixed with her blood in a tie-dye swirl of insanity.

"My dad wouldn't leave without me!" Bella's jaw clenched in a painful spasm that she rubbed gingerly.

Stella's sorrow turned into a cruel smirk. "I had plenty of boyfriends in my day. I was extremely popular. When I got pregnant, your love-crazy dad offered to marry me. I thought I loved him back for a while, but I was wrong. He left both of us. Good riddance, I say. Do your homework or whatever it is you do, and leave me alone."

Bella wrapped her coat tightly around her slim body. The glowing red trees brought the colder days and the hoped-for peace of the holidays. She sighed as she put the camera into her backpack while Stella stumbled into the house.

The last time Stella was here, she tried to run over Bella in their driveway. Dad had given her an ultimatum: get help, or they were leaving. After a year of full-time treatment, Stella was gone, and Mother came home. Although Mother lacked maternal warmth, things had been normal until now.

The high-pitched vibration of more breaking glass came from inside the old gray house, and it bruised Bella's soul. She turned away from where second chances had seemed possible and walked back down the tree-lined driveway.

When she got to the road, the boy was there again. Instead of going to town, she raced toward him. There was an overpowering musky smell, like the cologne her father wore.

"Please talk to me. My mother is sick and needs help."

He stopped for the first time but didn't turn around. "She killed me, you know."

"What?" Bella reached out to him, but he stayed out of her grasp.

"Run!" he screamed and disappeared.

The wheels of their van squealed down the driveway. Bella did what the boy told her—she ran.

"Time to join Daddy!" Stella screamed.

Bella veered off the road, hoping to make it to the forest and away from her crazed mother. An excruciating pain shot through her body. Then nothing.

Her father was kneeling next to her when she opened her heavy eyes. "You're safe now, my little Bella. I'm sorry I wasn't there to protect you."

Bella sat up, feeling no pain. "She's drinking again."

"I know, and she obviously stopped the meds and therapy. I can't believe I missed Stella's return." He buried his face in his hands.

"It's okay, Dad." Bella patted her dad's arm.

The boy hid behind her father. His hood was down, and he appeared to be about ten years old, with the most beautiful green eyes, messy brown hair, and a shy grin. She smiled and waved. He returned her gesture.

"Can you see the boy, Dad?"

He gathered Bella into his arms and held her as he used to when she was a child. "Yes. His name is Jake."

"Jake? You told me to run. Thank you."

Jake's smile faded, and a shadow crossed his face. "I failed you."

"How?" Bella frowned and met her father's brown eyes. He nodded toward the old cedar tree and flashing red lights. Their van had plowed into the tree, and her mother was being loaded onto a gurney. "Is she alive?"

"Yes. Her body will recover, but I'm not sure about her mind. I'm going to set you down now, if that's okay?"

"Sure, Dad. I feel fine."

Tears ran down Jake's face, and he put his hood back up. After a loud sniffle, he said, "Bella deserved to live, not that woman."

"I—" Bella stopped when her father pointed to the wreck. There was a familiar person between the car and the tree. "I'm dead?"

"Yes, sweetheart. We both are, but I think you'll like it where we're going. Right, Jake?"

Jake wiped his tears away. "Yes. It looks amazing, but I stayed here hoping to stop her from doing this again. It wasn't a deer your mom hit two weeks ago—she buried me over there." He pointed to a grove of trees next to the accident. "I was running away from one drunk mom and got killed by another. I hope they find my body someday. Even my mom deserves to know what happened."

Dad grabbed Bella's hand. "Time for all of us to go."

Jake scooped up her other hand, and they walked. Soon the world they left behind was forgotten as peace and love filled their souls. They entered a golden light where three beautiful angels waited for them. Their journey had just begun.

Deadline

THE NIGHT'S hand slowly gripped the forest. The house was unnervingly quiet after the winds stopped roaring through the trees. I sat at the computer, willing my fingers to fill a blank screen with clever words. A deadline loomed, but my cat, Max, demanded my attention, his claws firmly kneading my blanket-covered lap. I stroked his silky black fur as I ran through each idea and quickly rejected it.

My self-help blog had gone viral, and I needed a post for tomorrow. Although the blog helped me quit my banking job of twenty years and focus on writing and remodeling our newly purchased old farmhouse, it also provided a good deal of stress. Developing fresh and exciting material took a lot of work. With little time left over, I slowly increased the word count of my first romance novel. Being able to make a living by writing was a dream come true, but tonight I was in no mood to offer advice or even attempt to work on a love story —all because of a recurring dream. At first the dream was tame and flowed into my writing. It inspired my historical fiction romance, until it took a dark turn.

"It's a nightmare now, Max." The cat closed his eyes and settled into slumber.

I sighed and relived the dream again. It was always the same: a young woman from the past with crystal-blue eyes and blond hair in a single braid on her shoulder next to a startlingly beautiful face. She would be exquisite in any era but must have attracted a lot of attention in the 1800s. She wore a dark gray dress that was demurely cut and stood on the edge of a roaring river with longing in those innocent eyes. Then she removed a lavender ribbon from her hair and tossed it into the wind. The ribbon swirled and danced into the rapid currents that consumed it. It always ended here. I concluded she was longing for a lost lover, and that became my current love story.

That is until the story continued three nights ago. The woman followed a worn path to a gray stone cottage surrounded by a thriving vegetable garden and beautiful flowers. The house was silent as she added a log to the fire in the stone hearth. A black cooking pot hung above it. She dropped some potatoes and onions from her garden into the boiling water and plucked a chicken left on her counter.

Time blurred here in the dream—in the next part, she had a bowl in her hand. She dropped to the ground, clutched her stomach, and doubled over. "Help us, please. There is evil here." She crumpled to the ground like a rag doll, and I woke up.

Help her how? I didn't know who she—or "us"—was. It might only be a dream, but its tug continued when I was awake. Yet I kept it all inside since I couldn't find the words to explain what was happening to me, and I didn't want my love story to veer into horror. Hal knew about the first part of the dream, but what would my husband of twenty-five years think of the new twist? I already knew. He'd say I was working too hard. However, that wouldn't explain the foreboding that weighed me down.

This morning, there was a fresh addition. I experienced every labored breath of that young woman, who was now confined to a small, dark place. She had been buried alive.

"Write the truth, please. I am not possessed, but I will die here. Pray for my baby." Then it ended.

This had to stop. I attempted to tell Hal, but his attention was on his phone.

"Wow, honey. That sounds like a good mystery you're writing. I'd better pay some bills." He hurried down the hall with a slight wave.

Hal had been a great husband over the years, but he had a bad habit of not fully listening if I talked about something he wasn't interested in, like ghosts. I could have pursued it, and he would have been there for me, but I held back, knowing that even though I believed in the supernatural, would I have taken his dream seriously? No, I would not.

This inspired me to write a blog about journaling dreams and what you could learn from them. Despite my advice, I had yet to learn what to do with mine other than research. I spent the rest of the night studying local haunted houses and legends. I was about to give up my quest when my dream's tug amplified. *This was the house.* I had to go there and wanted—no, *needed*—Hal to go with me.

The following day, over coffee, I proposed the idea. "I've been researching haunted houses for my new book. There's one only an hour away that I'd like to explore. Wouldn't that be a fun way to spend Halloween?"

He smiled. "Downright spooky. I don't believe in all that otherworldly stuff, like the ghost hunter shows you watch, but I'll go for the ride."

"You don't have to believe to go on a spooky date with your wife. I want to write about a ghost who helps solve murders and brings couples together. This house has a great old cemetery, and I read there are two bodies buried outside it. I can't find any information about why or who they were. It sure has me thinking—what if they were still roaming the Earth, not being buried in the family plot? They could be my lovable crime-solving ghosts."

"You know I love a good mystery, and as long as I'm with you, I'm content."

Two days later, we pulled in front of the house. A painfully cold wave of recognition sped through me.

"I need to find a bathroom." I squeezed my hands together, digging my nails into my palms as sweat covered my body.

"You okay, Sadie?"

"Yeah, must have been something I ate."

"Well, not much around but this abandoned house. There was that fast food place we passed a way back. They'd have a restroom."

Relief washed over me as I made it there in time. I offered my best reassuring smile as I got back into the car with my worried husband.

"Maybe we should do this another day?"

I shook my head, "No, I'm fine. Can't eat that greasy food anymore."

Hal frowned but drove. Soon we were parked in front of the house again—thankfully, without my stomach reacting. The place reminded me of *The Addams Family*, minus the good-natured comedy my romantic side craved. The front windows were boarded, and the house's color had faded to gray. Behind it was a thick, untamed forest. Even at high noon, it looked like it was challenging us to come near it.

"Let's check it out." I hopped out of the car and pushed my way forward.

The rusty black front gate had a chain wrapped around it, but the lock was resting in the weeds. The house was still owned by the Pullet family, who lived on the other side of the country. Now that I look back, I wonder if that distance was intentional, although distance didn't seem to make a difference for me.

As soon as I crossed through that gate, my feet had a mind of their own. I grabbed Hal's hand and guided him through the overgrown rosebushes to the back of the house. We carefully walked through the meticulously aligned headstones. They dated back to 1820, when Henry Pullet died at thirty-nine years old. His wife lived to be seventy-five, and only one of their three children was buried here, at sixty. Her spouse and child were laid to rest next to her a few years later.

"Look at this small grave. So sad," I said.

Hal bent down to read the headstones. "Baby boy. Didn't name him or leave a date."

"That was fairly common back then." I tried to pretend the thought didn't hurt me, but my heart ached for that baby and his family.

"I'm glad our baby boy grew up into a man." Hal stood with a slight grunt.

I grabbed his hand and squeezed. "Me too. Just wish he wasn't in Germany."

"I'm sure he'll get leave soon and come visit us. Proud of him for serving our country." Hal's voice lowered in the familiar mixture of pride and worry that arose when he talked about our son's chosen path. I felt the very same way.

"Me too," I responded with a lump in my throat.

I was compelled to leave the graves and head outside the fenced area. I pushed through the overgrown bushes past another fallen fence, and there were two graves, marked with only initials.

I pointed. "These are the two graves I was reading about. Weird, huh?"

Hal frowned. "Didn't get much of a headstone. Maybe they worked for them?"

"Unlikely. They would have been buried at the local church, not here. This is more like where they put people who don't deserve to be in a sacred place with the others."

"Wonder if they were having an affair or something?" Hal pushed back the vines, but there was nothing else.

"Perhaps." My stomach tightened, and that same nausea passed over me. I bent down and threw up all over S. R.'s grave.

It got worse from there until I finally passed out. The next thing I knew, I was back in the car, and Hal was securing my seat belt.

I tried to sit up, but a wave of dizziness passed over me, so I stayed put. "How did I get here?"

Hal tossed his jacket over my lap and threw the car into drive. "I carried you. You passed out. I'm taking you to the nearest hospital."

My teeth chattered as the heat kicked on. "I'm sure they'll say it's a bug or something I ate."

Hal shook his head. "You *are* getting checked out. I've never seen you do that before."

"I don't need a doctor. It was like I was standing on evil."

Hal looked at me and frowned, but he didn't answer.

As predicted, I was told it was a bug and to go home and rest. Call if it gets worse. It didn't. I was fine when we pulled into our driveway and I saw the manicured lawn and a fresh coat of yellow paint on the old farmhouse.

"See, something I ate," I told Hal as he helped me out of the car.

"You are going to rest. We will watch a chick flick, and I'll make you some soup."

"I meant what I said back there." I sucked in the cold evening air as we headed inside the house. "The world was closing in on me over that grave. My dream . . . " I plopped down on the couch.

"You aren't sleeping enough. Of course you got sick." Hal threw a plaid blanket over me and crossed his arms. He wasn't listening again.

Three weeks sped by, and soon it would be Thanksgiving. That feeling of pure fear only intensified as the days passed. I tried praying, using holy water, smudging, and holding crystals while I remained busy writing. I knew something horrible had happened to those two people. Dark circles formed under my eyes from lack of sleep. I hid that under makeup, but my insides were worn down. Nothing I could pinpoint, just a heavy feeling that the spirits from those graves weren't at peace, and they'd somehow reached out to me. Why?

Last night, I finally fell into an exhausted sleep, and the dream took a horrifying twist.

I spent the next day walking around in a daze, trying to get that image out of my mind. When Hal got home late from work, he said,

"You're relapsing. I'm going to make some chicken soup and toasted cheese sandwiches."

He sat me on the couch while he whipped up our dinner.

"Well, that sure cured me," I told him with the biggest phony smile I could manage. "You should go to bed. I'm going to read on the couch for a little longer."

He wrapped another blanket around me and kissed my forehead. "You're freezing. Don't stay up too late."

"I won't. Night."

I sipped the tea with honey and lemon that Hal left with me. Instead of reading or writing my blog, I got on my cell phone and found nothing new about that young woman or the house. It was dead end after dead end. My head throbbed, and my world twisted in darkness. Then it consumed me completely. The next thing I knew, I had fallen on the floor and had a large lump on my forehead. On my phone screen was a picture of a barn—our barn.

We hadn't gotten around to fixing the abandoned barn since we moved into the house. I knew I had to go out there.

I pulled myself up and tugged on my coat.

"Hal?" I called softly, but gentle snoring continued in the next room.

Max was sleeping on the end of the couch. No one would miss me. I grabbed the flashlight and flipped on the outside lights that lit the area to the barn. This was one time I wished we had a dog along with our spoiled cat. It might be time we got one on our apple farm. Crime was almost unheard of here, but mountain lions weren't. I grabbed our handgun, tucked it into my waistband, and slipped into my boots and gloves.

The night was chilly, and there was a threat of snow. The ground crunched under my shoes, but the night was still—perhaps too still.

I went around the large double doors and opened the smaller entrance off to the side, where the farmers would check on their livestock. Farm animals hadn't been here in a few years, but their scent still lingered. The barn was used for storage now. When I found the switch, I prayed the old lights worked. One bulb came on, offering a reprieve from the heavy darkness.

"What am I doing? Hal isn't going to like me prowling around this late at night. Heck, I wouldn't like him doing it, either. Maybe I should—"

That feeling passed over me again, and I couldn't finish those words. Or had I hit my head too hard? Another wave of sickness flowed over me, and I threw up on the scattered wisps of hay on the moldy wooden floor.

"Oh, God!" I bent over next to an old green trash can as the rest of my dinner came back up. As soon as the barn stopped spinning. I refocused on where I was. The previous owners had left cardboard boxes full of old Christmas ornaments on plywood boards in the rafters. The realtor had offered to remove them, but I insisted on keeping them. Never know what treasure they might contain. And now here they sat, three months later. A solid wood desk was worn from years of use. Two drawers were empty, and the third one was locked. On the wall was a cascade of keys, only one small enough to fit. I tried it—it opened.

"Well, I'll be. It's an old journal with a note tucked inside."

Honey, this is your Aunt Sarah's diary. I found it after she passed and her husband Thomas took their son William back east to his family's home. They never came back. We rented the house after that, thinking her son might want it when he grew up because I certainly wanted nothing to do with it. I always felt it was cursed. The checks were sent to him, and his father hired someone to take care of it and the tenants. I only hung on to the holiday decorations in the barn rafters. It didn't seem right to toss away something that might hold good memories. The journal, well, I couldn't throw it away even though I had no interest in reading it. After a horrible nightmare, though, which I won't go into details about, I knew it had to be read someday. You decide if you're the one to read it. Heed my warning. Stay away from that side of the family and that house. Never know if your aunt's obsession passed on to her son, but it's still in that house. The crazy woman even had head-stones and graves put next to her that her husband and son never used. I now wonder if I should have reburied your aunt Samantha and her husband, Finnegan Ryan, but at the time, it seemed best to let them rest in peace where they were. I know I never talked to you about my family, but if you want to know, here it is, Catherine.

Love always,

Father.

A chill rushed through me with the power of lightning. We bought this house in an estate sale from two daughters after the mother died. Catherine Jones was the name of the mother. That couldn't be a coincidence. Now it made sense—descendants of the Pullets had lived here.

I paged through writing that had faded or smudged until I found pages that were virtually pristine, in a flowery hand that I assumed was Sarah's. I pointed the flashlight at the book and began reading.

My sister, Samantha Rose Pullet Ryan, is responsible for the death of her baby boy. People say she drowned him and then burned him. They also say that after that, she and her husband consumed poison. I know what happened, though. I know their evil and the demons that lived in all of them. Samantha was never right in the head, and I believe she was easy for evil to enter, and she drew an evil Catholic husband to her. It certainly wasn't natural how men flocked to her, and then she picked the one my beloved and devoted Baptist mother hated. People bought Samantha's sweet act, including Mother, but I didn't. No one is that pure and sweet. Samantha had her pick of the best men in town, but she chose a poor teacher. I saw he was like her in his insipid blue eyes and that horrid blood-red hair. Evil.

The words from the past pounded me. It was unnerving how crazed Sarah sounded. I turned the page and found a single picture of two girls. The girl from my dreams! The back said they were

Samantha and Sarah. Samantha looked happy and full of life next to her older, painfully plain sister. I sighed and continued reading.

With our father dead over ten years, our mother under my sister's spell, and my brother Richard Jr. still full of youth, I took charge as the head of our family. I did what needed to be done. No one speaks Samantha's name now after what they think happened, and I let them believe it. Mother, Richard, and I would be dead if I hadn't acted. We buried Samantha with her low-life husband outside our family plots. They didn't deserve to be placed with our family. That unfortunate baby had the same demons inside as the parents. Why, he didn't even have a proper American name! Who names a boy Devlin? Evil was in his name. Still, I couldn't talk Mother out of burying her grandson beside my father. She had an angel made for him to protect his soul in eternity. She believed Samantha would come after him again if she could, but I knew better. We needed to worry about ourselves. To be safe, I sprinkled holy water on his grave every day. No one understood, but I knew. Samantha's beauty was only a shell hiding the evil inside of her. She spent years sucking the life out of me so she could be so lovely. But I can marry Thomas with her gone, since he won't be under her spell. I wished I had more time to burn all of them, but freeing Devlin was more important. My clueless little brother turned eighteen last week and announced he was buying land and starting a farm with the money our father had left him. He told me to keep the house. He never was bright. Good riddance, I say. No one understood what I had to do. It was God's work.

I gasped and paged through the rest of the journal. There was nothing more to read. She killed her sister and family! I carefully tucked the diary back into the drawer. I knew what I needed to do. I had to speak for Samantha because her brother hadn't.

The barn shook like an elephant hit the side, but there was no damage. The heaviness, though, was lifted. The truth would stop those dreams, and I had plenty of material for my blog about trusting yourself.

I went back into the house and sat at my computer. The pages flowed as I introduced an insane murderer and her victims. I knew that Samantha was finally free.

The Last Ride Of The Night

THE MONSTERS REMAINED in the shadows, waiting. My husband and I sat at the top of the Ferris wheel. I would have enjoyed the view any other time, but not with death lurking below us. Pete wrapped his arm protectively around my shoulders as the last hopeless scream faded away. It was the older man who operated the ride, the same man who had winked at us and said we had the wheel all to ourselves because it was almost closing time. We didn't even know the name of the hero who had stopped the ride right before—

No, I couldn't think about that.

I tried to dial 9-1-1, but there was no signal. I couldn't text or email. There was no way to communicate or get information.

"We're safe up here, Lacy."

"What if they climb up?"

"These creatures can barely walk. They're like zombies."

I nodded, watching the monsters approach a building where a family had taken shelter. I'd seen that beautiful family in line when we got our favorite chocolate swirl ice cream in a cup. The two young boys had been so excited about their first monster truck show. I hoped the actual monsters didn't find them now.

Our car swayed, and my hand dug into Pete's leg.

"What if they knock the wheel down?" My mouth was so dry that the words barely escaped.

"It's too heavy. Don't worry, sweetheart." Pete handed me my water bottle. The cool liquid soothed my throat.

Words spilled out of me. "All I can do is worry. How can we not? We were enjoying our night at the fair. Heck, we even danced to our song. If we hadn't had to ride this thing, we'd be safe in our car escaping this . . . whatever it is. These things came out of nowhere, and it feels like we're in a horror movie. This can't be real. Do you think it's all a show?"

For the first time, hope surged through me. Yes, it wasn't real.

Pete's mouth tightened. "I wish it weren't real—I do. You saw what they did. They . . . "

Tears overflowed my eyes as I glanced at the dark forms on the ground by the cinnamon roll cart. Thankfully, the glow of the colorful fair lights missed them, yet by the position of their legs and arms, it was apparent their bodies weren't intact. I shuddered as my fear overflowed until there was nothing left. Pete put his head on top of mine, and we held each other, listening to the screams and car horns.

"Many people got away. And surely help is coming." I sniffled as Pete handed me a fresh Kleenex—he always kept one tucked away in his jean pocket.

A rumble was headed in our direction. It was a helicopter! It hovered over the fair, shining its light. Soon another one joined it.

"We're saved!" I cried.

Pete stood, waving frantically as the car swayed.

A voice came over the loudspeaker as a siren flashed in the distance. "We see you, sir. Remain seated. We will get you out of there."

"Thank you!" Pete called, but they didn't hear his voice over the rapid gunfire.

The monster's bodies piled up quickly. Three men and a woman rappelled down yellow ropes. I had never been happier to hear a steady rain of bullets.

"There's one! Look out!" A woman's voice screamed over the terror.

Another barrage of popping, and then it stopped. The doors to the photography building where that family had hidden opened. I was relieved that they exited safely. The Ferris wheel lurched into motion.

"It's over!" I cried. Pete and I hugged.

"I told you it would be okay up here."

I was never so glad to stand on damp grass. Soldiers wearing gas masks rounded up survivors.

"Attention!" a loud voice boomed, and everyone fell silent.

"There has been a bioattack on your community and others like yours. Those who have no symptoms in the morning will be taken into quarantine. We will offer you a protective vaccine at that point. Food, water, and blankets will be provided after you check in."

Pete took my hand. He never let go of me as we listened to gunshots and tractors removing the infected victims. We survived the night, but many didn't. After being disinfected, we left behind a town we'd never see again. They relocated us into whatever the new normal had become.

Faith

For Desiree

NESSIE STOOD ON THE MOUNTAINTOP, her arms extended in gratitude toward where she believed heaven existed. Only her faith had brought her to this moment. If she hadn't felt the possibility of survival, she would still be tied up in that dark, musty room at the mercy of a madman. She shuddered thinking of those dire moments.

"I'm free!" she shouted. She twirled around, offering her thankfulness.

Her voice echoed through the rocky canyons. There would be no response to her glee—this was a journey she'd made alone. It was her time to shine and celebrate her strength. She settled down and meditated on the beauty. She bowed her head in thanks when she was done. Opening her backpack, she removed a turkey-and-avocado sandwich.

"Thanks, Mom. This is the best sandwich yet!" She smacked her lips.

Soon her meal was concluded, and the pack became a back rest to watch the sun push the day away with its brilliant purple, pink, and red finale.

"Goodnight, sun. Tomorrow you will rise again, as I did." Nessie shook her head and jumped up. "Everyone thought I was crazy to come up here alone, where it all happened. They don't understand. I promised I would experience the sunrise over this mountain if I survived. I prayed on that, and here I am honoring those words."

She unwound her sleeping bag in a spot that looked like it was made to sleep on and yanked on her coat and hat as the air chilled and the stars came out. Stargazing was her favorite thing to do as a child. She was a part of the universe on the cliff where a man had killed her fiancé, Steve, and taken her hostage. The place where she had declared she would get married someday. It had always been her favorite spot.

"No, that man didn't ruin this beauty for me. He couldn't."

That man didn't know that this place was magical, and Steve hadn't believed in it as she did. The push from the cliff had snapped his neck, but it didn't end his journey. His spirit stuck around long enough to help her after that insane man beat her and locked her up. She knew Steve would come to her. He held and comforted her. If not for him, she would never have spotted the dropped key in the dark.

"Thank you, Steve."

The rest was her, however. Once she got out of her prison, she had to get past her tormentor. Every step had pained her. That man had amused himself with every part of her, but nothing had been broken, so she had done what she needed to do.

"I'm so glad everyone thinks I got hurt trying to get to Steve. It's for the best, especially for my parents. They'll never have to suffer or know what I endured. Plus, I made sure it would never happen again."

Nessie smiled and closed her eyes in the sleep of peace. She slept soundly until her phone alarm woke her up. She quietly ate her granola bar and drank water as the sun rose from above the tree line behind her. The morning beams wove into the chill mountain air and offered her the beautiful rays of light that painted a new day. She took picture after picture to remember this glorious moment. The battery was at 10 percent, so she shut her phone off.

After cleaning up the campsite, she packed up and offered a final bow to the beautiful landscape. Standing on the edge of her new life, she released Steve's ashes over the precipice. Then she headed back down the mountain. When she entered the darkness of the tree canopy, she found the hidden path to a small log cabin. It was so off the beaten path that no one else knew it was there.

"Hi, honey, I'm home," she called out, smiling.

The place was cold, so she warmed up the red plaid décor, the deer heads mounted on the walls, with a nice roaring fire. She gathered food and a blanket and opened the trap door under the bear rug by the hearth. Clicking on the flashlight and tucking it under her arm, she clutched the cold metal handrail. In her free hand, she clasped Steve's handgun.

She shone the narrow light beam on a man huddled in the corner between the metal toilet and sink. He was crying.

He held his hands together in prayer form. "Please help me," he said in a whiny voice. "I'm dying."

His act didn't move her. "Not yet. Here are some supplies. Make them last a while. It's hard to say when or if I can get back here again with the snow coming."

He put his bearded face into his grimy hands. "I'm sorry I hurt you and your friend. I promise I'll never do it again."

Nessie smiled. "Oh, I know you won't, because you aren't leaving this room."

He looked up. His watery blue eyes still held that coldness she'd seen while he was enjoying hurting her. "I've never done that before. I was drunk."

She set the basket down out of his reach. "Good try, Larry. I found the graveyard out back and the holes for Steve and me. We weren't your first."

"Please, turn me in." He eyed the basket, and drool ran down his chin.

She shone the light on his goodies. "I think this fits the crimes. Plus, it gives you some time to think about what you did. Maybe you'll ask for that forgiveness you so desperately need. I'm doing you a favor in the long run."

"You're crazy." His voice took on a hardness that showed he didn't want redemption.

Nessie sighed loudly and kicked the basket within his reach. "Maybe I am now, thanks to you. The love of my life, who you took from me, brought me to this mountain to ask me to marry him. I have the ring next to my heart to remind me of my love and faith. It saved me. What will save you?"

"Please. You aren't like me." The chains rattled, but he had made no progress pulling them from the wall. She knew how well he'd installed them.

"No, I'm not. I'm doing good for the world right now. You'd better make your peace for all your sins."

Nessie shut the trapdoor and locked it. Relief overwhelmed her as she sank into a dusty red chair and let the memories surface. Had it only been three weeks ago? She had unlocked her chains with the dropped key. She prepared herself to fight him but found the house empty, except for the smug man's tranquilizer gun. Still, she didn't run. She waited for him to return. He tried to fight her, so she shot him. After she dragged the sedated body to his prison, she used the same chains that had been on her and left him where he'd put so many before. In that dark hole, she put several boxes of granola bars, raisins, and nuts by his unconscious body. He had a water supply.

She forgot her pain as she searched the house and surroundings. There were so many graves, all marked with numbers. Two empty holes meant for her and Steve. They would have been numbers 16 and 17. That was when Steve appeared to her for the last time.

"I will always love you, Nessie. Would you do one more thing for

103

me?" She nodded, so he continued. "Make sure he gets what he deserves, sweetheart."

"I promise. I love you too, and I'll miss you."

Then he waved and faded away without another word into a bright, golden light. She made the painful trek back down the mountain and decided not to tell anyone what had happened to her and Steve. Someday she'd alert the authorities anonymously so those other families could find some closure, but she needed to find hers first.

This time inside the cabin, she was much stronger and knew she needed to eliminate any evidence that she'd been there. There were some gloves in his cleaning supplies, and she scrubbed the cabin to her satisfaction. She removed the gloves and tucked them into her pocket.

"Good luck, Larry. If you're meant to live, you will. If not, you have some things to pay for."

She hoped he would be thankful for her kindness in leaving him supplies, but she doubted it. Someone like him wouldn't recognize empathy—he hadn't shown her any when he used that belt.

Another trip down the mountain. Nessie left her greatest love and her fear behind, but she was filled with faith for the life she had yet to live.

When The Clock Stopped

99 Words

WHEN I TOOK my first breath, the delicate porcelain clock trimmed in gold had stopped running at exactly 4:08 a.m.

"You were my miracle," Mother would say, dusting the clock no one was allowed to touch.

Now it sits on my mantel. My grandson tried to fix it, but the motor and the clock's arms wouldn't budge.

Today I woke up feeling unwell. I picked up the phone to call my doctor when I caught the gentle ticking. The clock was running.

Then everything disappeared into a golden glow, and I found myself gathered in my mother's arms again.

The Day The Ground Moved

IT JOLTED me from a deep sleep, and my belongings were tossed around like feathers in a windstorm. My wedding picture crashed into the back of my head, but I had no time to worry about the bump as I rode my bed to the dresser lodged on its side. My black cat, Sissy, dug her claws into my leg, and my poor dog was howling from his bed.

"It's okay, Astro!"

It was unlikely the dog heard me over the snarl of the shifting landscape and shattering glass. I pulled myself to the side of the bed as Sissy edged up to my chest.

"Hang on. It's a big one."

Clutching the cat, I slipped on the leather mules my wife of thirty years had given me last Christmas. Losing Nancy three months later to breast cancer crushed my soul, but a small part of me was grateful she missed the next cruel chapter in our world. I pushed down my pain, grabbed our wedding picture, and attempted to run. The floor rolled like a carnival funhouse, and I could barely keep upright. My stomach flipped as a powerful wave surged through the house. I grabbed the closet door frame.

"I should take the go-bag, Sissy." She buried her head in my neck.

I gripped the wooden structure tightly with one hand, snatched the bag from the closet, tucked the picture in it, and slung it over my shoulder. Sissy's claws deepened, cutting into my skin, but the pain barely registered as I navigated the dark hall to the creaking steps. The rising sun peeked through the broken front window, and a neighbor's car alarm was screaming.

I clung to the shaking railing and crept down the wooden stairs. Halfway there, the wall cracked open with a loud pop. I raced down the rest of the stairs without looking back.

"Astro! Come!"

The sweet German shepherd inched to me with his tail between his legs. I clutched his collar.

"It's safer outside." I tried the front door. It wouldn't open until I used my ample weight against it. We burst onto the porch and raced out into the dawn. I bent over on the front lawn, gasping as the brick fireplace crumbled with a dusty thump on the side of the house.

"Is this ever going to stop?"

As if on cue, the Earth's seizure ended.

A familiar voice shouting for help from across the street broke through the car alarms. The two-level house was now one, and my neighbors and friends were inside that.

"I'm coming, Bert!"

The young couple who had moved in last month stood pale and bloodied by their shrilling car.

"Bert and Kate need help!" I yelled to them, waving. I set Sissy down, and she dove under my car.

The husband shook his head. "Sorry, we need to get to a safe zone. It would be best if you headed there too. They promised to welcome those who joined them with no punishment." They got into their car.

"Wait! There isn't—" Their car headed down the street. "Guess they'll find out."

When you get some birthdays behind you, empty promises

become very clear. There was no safety for any of us. In the distance, there was smoke and rubble as far as my old eyes could see—our "punishment." A loud screech and a blaring horn tugged my attention back to the foolish couple. Their shiny new electric car was half in and half out of a large hole. The husband pulled the wife out, and they disappeared around the corner.

"Good luck. You'll need it." I shrugged as Astro wagged her tail.

"Stay here, Astro." I patted her head, tightened my bathrobe belt, and headed to help my friends.

"Adam, can you hear me?"

"Yes, Bert. Hang on. I'll get you guys out."

Thankfully, he was in a pocket by the front door. I lifted the debris with a crowbar. Bert's wife, who had been Nancy's best friend, was crushed under a beam. We buried her under her favorite maple tree with the autumn leaves dropping, much like Bert's tears. I kept a comforting hand on his shoulder. It was all I could offer. I knew that pain when you lose your better half. There was no comfort.

Bert, Astro, Sissy, and I took over the only house left relatively intact—the one the young couple hadn't returned to. Bert's old ham radio and my generator survived, and we found a renegade radio channel. The news was dire. Part of our state was in the ocean, all because our area leader had challenged the new world directive. We refused to give up our weapons. The broadcaster confirmed that we were the cruel example of what would happen if you didn't do things the directive's way. Not only did they cause a massive earthquake by powerful fault detonation, they killed those seeking safety in their camps. It was war, and I knew the young couple would never make it home.

One side fought the other, with our side sorely limited in what we could do. Bert and I had a healthy supply of food, water, and weapons. Two old men, a dog, and a cat now lived in a world with no help, only enemies. When the time came, I would defend our old ways against the new directive. I knew Nancy would be proud of my stand, but I couldn't wait to be with her again—when that time came.

A Day At The Lake

THE HAZY SUNBEAMS vanished under Lake Vera's icy surface as a bald eagle dove and captured a rainbow trout. The bird and its victim soared to a padded nest on top of the cedar. Cathy snapped shot after shot on the camera she'd saved all year to buy. The heavy new lens gave her a close-up of the steely determination in the eagle's eye and the blood seeping from the squirming fish. The eaglets would eat well tonight.

On a red plaid blanket, Cathy sat as still as the alert deer with her fawn drinking from the water's edge. She slowly turned the camera on the gentle creatures, adding to her growing collection of nature shots. When the deer finally got their fill of the algae-ridden water, they disappeared into the tree's shadows. She took a break from photography and pulled out the carefully packed roast beef sandwich with mayo, mustard, pickles, and lettuce on a sourdough roll—*all the fixings*, as her mom used to say before she faded away into dementia.

After finishing her meal, she wiped her mouth with a soft red cloth napkin that smelled of spring. She cleaned up her area to reflect her love of nature. As the sign said, *Pack it in, pack it out*. It had been the perfect day to go to the lake and have it all to herself. Today was how Cathy had pictured retirement, but until now, she'd spent it as her mother's sole caretaker, which was the real reason she was here.

"Goodbye, Mom. I hope you find some peace now."

She bent down at the lake's edge and released the ashes. This was the place her family had come for summer picnics. Now Cathy was the only one left. She snapped pictures of what remained of her childhood, slowly floating away on the mirror-still lake toward the bald eagle's nest and the creepy old oak tree.

She shook her head, pulled herself up, and brushed off the leaves, dirt, and crumbs. "Seems like you're still trying to get to that tree, Mom. I never understood why you liked that mangled oak so much."

She remained in contemplation for a few more minutes before turning to go. A tremendous splash from the lake landed a few drops on her hand. She turned, thinking a tree had fallen, but the lake only provided the aftermath of waves from an unknown event.

"The ashes are gone!" Cathy's heart quickened, and her instinct to run was overruled by her curiosity.

Glowing green cat eyes peered from the water, and the smell of rotting fish overwhelmed her with dizziness. She dropped to her knees as the eyes that now mesmerized her moved closer to shore.

She gasped. "What the—"

At that moment, the bald eagle dove past the hypnotic eyes but quickly retreated to the sky when the lake appeared to reach for it. A hairless, misshapen gray head broke the water's surface and paused like a dog on a leash. Its eyes narrowed as the massive, alligator-shaped mouth showed its teeth and its unhinged, snakelike jaw opened wide. Those few seconds brought her back to reality.

Cathy bolted forward like she was at the starting gate at a track meet. She abandoned her backpack and pumped her legs faster than they had moved in over twenty years. Her camera bounced against her chest like a jackhammer. It would leave bruises, but that was the least of her worries. She raced up the hill to where the well-trodden trail started. A roar echoed across the lake as water battered the shore. Heavy, gloppy steps on the rocky beach followed.

Cresting the hill, she refused to look back. The stories about the lake monster were true. That thing had ingested her mother's remains, and now it wanted her.

A gentle voice cut through the distance. It sounded a lot like her mother. "Wait, Cathy. I only want to say goodbye."

Cathy hesitated as long-overdue tears filled her eyes. She couldn't fight the powerful urge to turn around anymore. The rays of the orangey-gray sunset broke through the heavy clouds and offered a well-lit picture of a nightmare. It was not her mother. Without thinking, she snapped a shot of what was before her.

"Sweetheart, what's wrong? It's me." Laughter gurgled out.

The thing crept closer. Two long, pallid tentacles jutted out like arms and left behind a slimy trail like a snail on whatever they touched. The neon eyes gleamed with madness, and its wrinkled, serpentine form was expanding on legs the same size as her body.

Cathy's whole body shook. Her heart couldn't take too much more of this, or at least that's what the doctor had told her last week. "No! Stay away from me!"

She ran up the trail, careful not to trip over anything. The sucking sound followed.

Why did I come here alone?

"Cathy!"

She kept running, breathless, as the night encroached. Luckily, her cell phone and keys were in her pocket, not in that abandoned backpack, and it wasn't much farther to her Jeep. Sweat trickled down her face, and a pain in her chest threatened to slow her down. She didn't have the luxury to indulge in her discomfort.

"Doesn't. It. Need. Water?" She panted now like an old dog.

Relief coursed through her as she reached the parking lot, where only one vehicle sat—hers. The sucking sound stopped, and the pain in her chest subsided. One beep opened the driver's door. She jumped inside and pressed the lock with an enormous sigh of relief.

"What. Just. Happened?" Hopeful, she glanced at her phone—no signal. "No one will believe me. Even with a picture."

She set the camera on the passenger seat and inserted her key. There was only a *click*.

"The battery is dead? Are you kidding me?" Cathy hit the steering wheel and burst into tears as the sucking sound started again.

Pain exploded in her chest, and the Jeep door popped open. Darkness shrouded Cathy and silenced her weak cries.

* * *

Three weeks later, Brad nervously drove his Camaro to Lake Vera to drink beers with his best friend, Randy.

Randy pointed with the light from his cell phone as he exited the car. "Dude, there's a camera by that old Jeep."

Brad's arms filled with goosebumps as he slipped on his head-lamp and followed Randy to investigate. "The keys are right here, and no one is inside. But the smell . . . Let's get out of here. I think the lake monster was here."

Randy shook his head, swirling his long brown hair like a ballerina's tutu in Brad's light beam. "There's no such thing as a lake monster. I keep telling you that. But something bad happened here. I bet it was a serial killer. Maybe this camera has a clue. Let's party somewhere else, dude, and figure it out later."

Both were safely back in the car with the doors locked when Brad exhaled loudly. "That's a dead smell. We need to call the cops."

Randy ran his fingers through his hair and popped open a beer. "They'll ruin our good vibe, but it's your car, so whatever."

"Hey, don't drink while I'm driving!"

Randy chugged the beer and tossed it outside. "Done."

Brad rolled his eyes at his childhood friend and put his car into gear as a booming female voice came from the darkness. "Wait, come back! I need a ride home."

"Let's go. We'll make that call." Randy urged his friend.

Brad couldn't ignore someone in trouble. He rolled down his

window and squinted into the moonless night. "You need help, ma'am?"

"I sure do. Boy, am I glad to see you. My Jeep broke down."

Randy leaned out of the window. "Where are you?"

"Right over here. I hurt my ankle and could use some help." Neon-green eyes cut through the darkness.

Randy grabbed Brad's arm. "Do you see those eyes, dude? They aren't human. Drive!"

A loud sloshing sound sped toward them.

"We'll send help back, ma'am!" Brad stomped on the blue Camaro's gas pedal.

The wheels squealed in protest against the asphalt as something held the car in place. Hollow laughter filled the parking lot as Brad and Randy screamed.

* * *

It was over as quickly as it began, and then the night was heavy with welcome silence. The two empty vehicles became dessert. It had been a feast, and it was time for a very long sleep. Vera slowly made her way back to her lake, only stopping once to dine on a lovely deer family. She let out a loud burp that rumbled the ground beneath her and then sank back into the icy water.

Living creatures offered her the blood she needed, but the cars added some friendly fiber that would take years to digest. Metal, oil, plastic—nothing hurt her. Vera burrowed into the muddy lake bottom, where she'd digest everything over the next several decades. She could relive the lives of all the consumed humans and animals in her dreams, like those movies they so enjoyed. Satisfied, Vera closed her eyes until she needed to feed again.

The Bike

Twelve-year-old Billy started his day filled with the Christmas spirit. He took the Number 3 bus to downtown Laceyville. Barely a dot on the map, but it was where you went if you needed something. Mom was working her last shift at the small diner down the road. Little Joey stayed with old Mrs. Trumbold, who had a never-ending supply of sugar cookies and milk. On special occasions, she'd add some chocolate chips to the cookies.

Billy sat in the middle of the bus. There were only two other people sitting in the back. Everyone minded their business, so he enjoyed the holiday decorations through the scratched-up window. Every house had a tree in the front window covered in silver tinsel and colored lights. The bus jolted to a stop right in front of Harvey's Department Store. Billy clutched his dingy sock full of change and dollar bills and followed a sour older man who smelled of horse manure and cheese to the bus's side door. The man eyed him like Billy might knock him down.

The store was glowing. Covered in red and green holiday decorations, it was full of last-minute shoppers. His mom had brought him and his little brother here to take in the holiday cheer and visit Santa a few weeks ago. He knew Santa was hired help in a red suit, but Joey still believed in all that magic. Billy wisely asked for new clothes, knowing he'd be lucky to get that, but Joey requested a new red bike.

His mom's eyes filled with tears after looking at the bike's price tag. He knew twenty-five dollars was more than she could afford. She didn't make that much working at the diner, where tips were meager. At least they'd get some chocolate candies in their stocking and a warm secondhand coat.

Billy had been earning extra cash mowing lawns and cleaning garages over the last several months. His mom wanted to take him to the bank and start a savings account, but he was halfway to getting the Sting-Ray bike all his friends had. Of course, none of that mattered now because Billy became the man of the house after his father died from cancer eleven months ago. He would use his money to get his little brother what he'd asked Santa for and have enough left to get Mom something nice, like his dad used to do. He could always earn enough to get what he wanted by next summer.

Billy dodged a large woman whose arms were filled with toy trucks and dolls. Lucky kids. He headed to where the bikes were, but the red one was gone. In its place was a blue model that was ten dollars more—eight more dollars than he had.

"Look out, kid." The lady pushed past him. "I'll take that bike too," she told the smiling saleswoman, who was dressed as Mrs. Claus.

"You are fortunate! That's our last bike."

Billy stood in line and inquired about the display bike in the window.

Mrs. Claus patted his head. "That has a dent on it, son. We need to fix it in Santa's workshop before it can be sold."

Billy shook his head. "A dent is okay. I have twenty-five dollars for it."

The woman reached around him and grabbed a scarf from a lady holding a screaming baby. "Sorry, that's against store policy. It would make the store look bad to sell damaged inventory. Buy something else. I have customers to wait on."

Billy sighed loudly. Joey would be so disappointed. Still, he was determined to add a few gifts under the decorated fig tree. A turquoise scarf and gloves set with a peacock feather design would be perfect for his mom, along with pink slippers, a robe, and a cheesy romance novel. He found a fire truck, a football, a new adventure book, new Christmas PJs, and slippers for his brother. The family always used to wear matching PJs on Christmas Eve, way back when life was normal and cancer hadn't taken away all its joy.

He added a package of SweeTarts to his purchases. That left him with enough change to ride the bus home. But when he stepped on the Number 3, he found the change gone and a hole in his pocket.

"No money, no ride." The red-haired driver had not been gifted with the Christmas spirit.

Billy bowed his head and retreated in embarrassment from the bus where no goodwill existed.

He ran to the store to look for his lost change, but the door was locked. A young man with braces and a red Santa hat took the dented bike out of the window display, ignoring Billy's pounding on the door.

"Guess I'm walking home."

Billy took the shortcut that passed the back of the store. The employee who had ignored him brought the bike out the back door. He tugged on the door that said Do Not Enter.

"Great, it's locked!" He dropped the bike and stomped back into the store.

The dim lights illuminated the red bike like it was on display. It would be perfect for his little brother. Billy pushed his bags full of gifts on his shoulders and did something he'd never done before. He stole the bike.

He had almost escaped the dark lot when a male voice screamed. "Stop, thief!"

Billy's stomach was heavy, but all it took was the thought of his brother's face on Christmas morning. His long legs kept pedaling on the small bike. Although he was a criminal now, he tried a deal he thought God might accept. "Please forgive me. If you let me keep it for Joey, I promise to pay the store back more than they were charging."

Turning onto the main road, he wove in and out of traffic. The icy wind pounded his face, and his thin coat offered no protection from the approaching winter storm. He tried to convince himself that what he had done was okay until guilt crashed down on him.

"Sorry, Joey. This isn't right."

Billy turned the bike around in the intersection as a bus barreled around the corner with its horn blaring. Everything in front of him went black except for a beautiful angel with long, ebony hair and sea-green wings.

That was the last thing he remembered until he smelled cheese, garlic, and bread. He carefully opened his eyes, expecting the angel again, but a kind-faced man was at his side.

Billy blurted out his story while the man gently shook his head and rubbed his chin but withheld comment.

"I've got to get the bike back to them, sir. It doesn't belong to me."

The man smiled. "That bike is dinged up, but it's yours."

Billy wondered if he was dreaming. "It's what?"

"My friend Officer Doyle told me you took it. I figured you had your reasons, so I offered to pay. The store manager gladly accepted. Although you aren't allowed in the store anymore unless an adult accompanies you." His smile was as gentle as his eyes.

Billy's eyes widened. "Why would you do that, mister?"

The man, who had to be as old as his mom, patted his arm softly. "Everyone deserves a second chance, and a young man like yourself should be with his family on Christmas Eve, not in jail. And please call me Mr. Jones."

"My name is Billy, Mr. Jones. But I spent all my money on these probably ruined presents." Billy pointed to the two bags on the table next to the red bench he was lying on.

When he grinned, Mr. Jones had creases around his eyes like his dad. "Your gifts are fine—not even a scratch on the fire truck."

Billy held back tears. "How can I pay you back?"

"I could use help around here on Saturdays and maybe sometimes after school. You could work off your bike. If everything goes well, I'll hire you permanently."

"Really? Gee, that would be great!" Billy sat up and winced as his head throbbed more. He was sore, but everything worked.

Mr. Jones pointed to his head. "That bump on your head will hurt you for a while, but the doctor said you'd be fine."

Billy looked around. "A doctor was here?"

"Yes, picking up a pizza to take home. Very lucky he was here so you didn't have to go to the hospital."

"Yes, lucky. Thank you."

"You're welcome. Now get up slowly, Billy, and gather your things. I'll take you and that bike home."

Billy jumped down to a sticky red tile floor. "You don't have to do more, Mr. Jones. I can ride the bike home, and you can be with your family."

A sad look crossed the man's face. "I lost my wife last year in a car accident. We were never blessed with kids, so you would be doing me a favor if you allowed me the holiday cheer of being able to return you to your family."

"Sorry, Mr. Jones. My dad died too." Billy inspected the man. He wasn't horrible looking, and a widower too. Maybe . . .

When they pulled in front of his house, his mother was talking to a police officer.

Billy stepped out of the truck with a loud gulp. "You should meet my mom, Mr. Jones. I know she'd like to thank you for all your help."

"I—"

"Billy!" She engulfed him in a tight hug. "Are you okay? What were you thinking? You are grounded for two weeks—" She stopped when she saw Mr. Jones. "Officer Doyle told me what you did for him, Mr. . . . ."

"Jones, but call me Mike. It was my pleasure to help." His new friend's brown eyes twinkled, and Mom's cheeks took on an odd shade of pink.

"My name is Maria. Nice to meet you, Mike." She held out her hand, which Mr. Jones engulfed in his large ones. The handshake went on longer than most.

"Nice to meet you, Maria. You raised him well. He was going to make things right after doing something so stupid. With your permission, he's agreed to help at my restaurant to pay off his debt. The road wasn't so kind, but the bus missed him. He's a fortunate young man."

"We were extremely lucky tonight, thank you. And of course you have my permission. I made a fresh pot of coffee. Would you like a cup?" Mom smoothed her wavy, dark brown hair and smiled.

Mr. Jones finally let go of his mom's hand as Officer Doyle walked by and waved. "Don't do that again, young man. You won't get so lucky next time. Happy holidays."

"I won't, sir. Merry Christmas!" Billy said.

Officer Doyle shook his head and winked at Mr. Jones before getting into his car.

"Good advice, Billy. I don't want to impose on your family celebration, Maria. Maybe another—"

Billy interrupted him before he could decline, much to his mom's obvious embarrassment.

"Mr. Jones is alone. Can't we invite him to our Christmas Eve dinner tonight?"

Her face relaxed. "It would be an honor if you joined us. Our way of paying back your kindness."

Mr. Jones nodded as Joey raced out of Mrs. Trumbold's house and threw himself into Billy's aching arms. Mr. Jones retrieved the bike, wrapped in a blanket, and followed Billy's mom into the garage.

The dent and the scratches went unnoticed Christmas morning, and it turned out to be a good Christmas, even though Billy missed his dad. Mr. Jones stayed for that dinner too and many more to follow.

Money worries became a thing of the past when Maria took over the paperwork in Mr. Jones's busy restaurant. It took over a year, but Mr. Jones became a part of the family. Maria cut back from working full-time to part-time after she announced they were expecting a baby, due on Christmas Day.

The baby arrived on the night when miracles happen—Christmas Eve. Not that anyone would believe it, but Billy saw the same beautiful angel standing next to his baby sister's crib, the one from the night the bus narrowly missed him. She smiled and waved at him, then disappeared.

Waiting

99 Words

EVERY NIGHT I stood on the edge of the precipice. My tears had stopped flowing, but the valley hadn't stopped burning. Everything was gone. Only my father had heeded the signs and prepared our escape. Unfortunately, he could only take my baby brother and sisters. He sent Mother and me to the mountain, promising to return. Mother never left the cave, but she kept our fire going. I caught fish and lugged our water from the icy stream. She insisted we were the only ones alive, but I believed. Tonight my dreams were answered as my father's balloon appeared.

The Clock

I GENTLY SHIFTED my weight in the chair, trying to pry my bare legs off the brown vinyl. Several deep breaths did nothing to relieve the tension in my shoulders. I pulled my sweater tightly around me, realizing it wasn't wise to be dressed for a hot summer day while sitting in a cold hospital room. There had been no change in the last few hours. The constant beeps continued, and the oxygen flowed in and out with a gentle *whoosh*.

I shook my head at the tragic irony of this man needing me after how he'd treated me growing up. My father had an undiagnosed mental condition. He hid it well. Only those who lived with him knew the explosive violence he kept under the mask of a family man. No one noticed the marks; they were never on my face. He was careful even when he lost control. The war and his parents had hurt him so deeply that when his pain bubbled to the surface, it hurt us. He never seemed aware of his faults, so there was never an opportunity for him to seek help. My family spent every waking moment trying not to upset him, hoping all would be well. It wasn't.

I sighed loudly and took a protein bar out of my purse. I wasn't hungry, but I didn't want to pass out and end up in a hospital bed too.

I washed the crunchy, honey-flavored oats down with a bottle of water. A nurse entered the room right after I finished. I pretended to be asleep. There was nothing new she could share with me.

When she was gone, I sat up, staring at the lump of a once proud and cruel man. We were the only two left of my family. Alcohol and drugs had taken everyone down except me. I knew when to quit. The man lying in bed had upped his drinking until it was all he did. Today I watched them remove twenty-one bottles of liquid from his abdomen, relieving his labored breathing. He didn't know it was happening.

A flash of light caught my attention, and I quietly got up to investigate. It was coming from the nurses' station. There was a small gold clock that looked like a holiday ornament, and the arms showed it was—

A chill shot through me.

It looked like the clock from my dream last night, in which I was boxing up my father's belongings. My only thought was that he wasn't dead yet. This exact clock showed up in one of the boxes. In the dream, it gently spun in a circle, playing my father's favorite Hank Williams Jr. song, showing me it was eight o'clock, like now.

"He was brought in today. How could I have seen it?" I whispered.

I headed back to my father's room, but a loud conversation stopped me from entering.

"Did you see what that patient in 202 left us today, Louise?"

"I've never seen a clock like that before. How sweet of him, and I love that song. Too bad it doesn't keep time."

I gulped. Unsure what to do, a sudden warmth wrapped me in its wisdom. I closed the door tightly behind me and stood over my father's withered body.

"I forgive you, Father, even after all you did to us. You weren't happy here on Earth, and I hope you'll find some happiness where you're going. Please know I'm doing this in love, and I believe it's what I was meant to do. Rest in peace."

I picked up the extra pillow and clapped it over his face. He never struggled, but at the last moment, his bloodshot eyes opened. There was approval in those brown eyes as the machines went silent. Finally, with a deep sigh, his eyes closed. I put the pillow back and pushed the nurse's button right as they threw the door open. Mercifully, they couldn't revive him.

Later, when I left his room, I hurried past the clock, still displaying the same time. During my long wait for the elevator, it played my father's favorite song, just like in the dream. I held back a smile when the minute hand moved to 8:03. That was my sign that everything was okay now.

There was no autopsy because he was expected to die. No one knew what I did that day. I was okay with that because he was free—and so was I.

Alone

THE DROUGHT HAD LEFT them all lazy. No one was prepared for a big storm as the heavy rains turned into snow the night before. Lydia had never minded being snowed in, even without power. But this time, with no power, internet, or communication, there was no joy, only anxiety. It was the first time in her life that she was entirely alone. The emptiness echoed loudly around her, bouncing off the carefully framed photos of happier times when living in a forest had been fun. There was only fear today when she went to leave the house and spotted an intruder. She quickly stepped back inside, slammed the door shut, and locked it. Wiping the frost from the front window, she peered through. They were still there. She tried waving, hoping they needed help, but there was no response except her goose-bumps and sweaty palms. Without Bill she had to survive what Mother Nature brought her and a trespasser.

She squinted, but the face was hidden in the shadows. She was convinced it was a man under forty from his brawny warrior stance. He wore faded blue jeans, a red plaid shirt, a black vest, and a black stocking cap, much like many of the men in their small community, including Bill. The snow boots were dated and reminded her of the ones they used to own. Moon boots, Bill called them. Misery coursed through her, thinking of her husband fighting for his life at the hospital while she couldn't get to him.

This person had to know she was alone and no one could help her. He must have watched the ambulance come and was aware there would be no 9-1-1 calls coming from her house—the power and phones had gone out right after. There was only the silence of a massive storm. She had not bothered to start the generator because she was planning to leave.

"Oh, Bill. I wish you were here. I warned you not to shovel the driveway. Pay the money and have the tractor do it. But no, you had to do it, and look at what it did to your heart."

She couldn't get that image out of her head—him down on his knees, clutching his chest. All she could do was keep him comfortable as he struggled to breathe.

"I love you," he had gasped and held out his hand.

They slammed the ambulance's back doors, ending any chance of response.

"I'll meet you there," she had told the youthful attendant.

"You can come with us. The roads are icy."

Oh, how she wished she had. But she had wanted her car and a change of clothes, just in case. When the power blinked off, she had the clothes in her backpack and her purse ready to go. She picked up the landline phone to call the hospital and let them know she was on her way, but it was silent. No dial tone.

Lydia sighed and locked the door behind her. She slipped onto the leather seat of their new SUV and inserted the key.

Click.

"Are you kidding me?" She tried and tried, but the engine wouldn't turn over.

Panic filled every part of her body. She had to get to her beloved husband. Slamming the door of the useless car, she remained at the end of the driveway, hoping to flag someone down to help her. No one drove by. Her one close neighbor was sitting on a beach, probably sipping a mai tai. The cell phone in her hand kept telling her sorry, there was no available network.

She went inside to layer on more clothes before making the long walk down the road to the Smiths' house. Nothing would stop her from being at her husband's side. Why hadn't she gone with him? But she couldn't change the what-ifs, so she picked up her backpack and purse and opened the door.

That had been an hour ago, and he was still there, standing in the shadows. She captured his picture on her cell phone but couldn't make out his face. Her camera with the telephoto lens had dead batteries, and there was no way to charge them. The lens wouldn't work. The binoculars only showed a blurry figure.

Yet there he stayed, like death was watching her.

She wouldn't allow him near her. It couldn't be her time. It couldn't be Bill's time, either. They still had places to explore.

Lydia allowed herself a small smile. "They must wonder where I am. I bet help is on the way." That idea had become her obsession since she abandoned her walk to the neighbor's house.

Reality crept back in, and she didn't know if she was a widow. That thought was a gut punch, but she had to believe that on some level, after forty-nine years of marriage, she would feel it if he wasn't there with her anymore.

The snow kept piling up, and no one came to check on her. Luckily Bill had brought an enormous stack of firewood inside. He always cared for her, and now she wasn't there when he needed her.

The man was still in his spot.

"What are you waiting for?" In frustration, she grabbed Bill's handgun and threw open the door. "What do you want?"

The man didn't respond.

"If you come near me, I will shoot you." She fired a warning shot off to the right.

The man didn't flinch, which sent chills through her body that even a wood fire couldn't touch. That shadowy figure had become the edge of her world. She shut the door, locked it, and started praying.

"Please, God, help me, and don't take Bill from me. I couldn't bear to lose him. I don't want to be alone. Let help find me."

She wrapped her fingers around the sapphire-and-diamond cross Bill had given her over thirty Christmases ago. This year he had given her a fluffy bathrobe and a new laptop. She got him a plaid flannel shirt and a new table saw. He always put unique jewelry in her sock, and this year was no different. A silver pine tree for her already heavy charm bracelet.

They had everything they needed—especially each other—and had never been apart since they met at her best friend's wedding over fifty years ago. They married six months later.

Her only regret was that they never had kids. She lost six babies, and they decided it wasn't meant to be. But with Bill, her life was full of joy and laughter.

She picked up a picture of the two of them in Italy, standing in front of the Leaning Tower of Pisa. They pretended to hold it up like everyone else, including a sweet young couple who took their picture.

"Hang on, Bill, I will find a way to you."

"Lydia."

"What? Who said that?"

She rushed to the window, relieved the man was still outside.

"I'm hearing things." She shook her head, and pain exploded inside it. She grasped her skull and sank to the ground. "Great, a migraine."

Too dizzy to stand, she crawled to the couch and pulled herself up. With a loud sigh, she collapsed on her side, teeth chattering. It was like the storm was inside of her. She couldn't get her left hand to pull the brown forest-patterned comforter over her, so she reached with her right hand. Her vision was dimming, as it usually did with the headaches, but there was no burst of colors at the edges, only darkness.

She sucked in air, but it felt like breathing through a narrow straw. She'd never had a migraine this bad before. Of course, with the stress of Bill's heart attack, she wasn't surprised. The couch was so soft she couldn't shift her body to lie flat. Probably better to stay this way until it passed.

The pain was subsiding, and she was so sleepy. Her tongue was heavy, and there was a burned smell like a piece of food had fallen on the wood stove. She could barely hold her eyes open to see the man in the plaid shirt right in front of her.

She opened her mouth to scream, but nothing came out. Then it all faded away, and it was only her and Bill. They were together again, and he looked handsome—and so much younger—in the red plaid shirt she'd given him for Christmas. She took his offered hand. His warmth soothed her.

"Everything is going to be okay, sweetheart. I've been waiting for you. Remember how we never wanted to leave each other alone? Our prayers were answered."

Together they walked toward a beautiful golden light.

Effervescent Potion

For Jeffry

THE ROUND MAN in the white lab coat dropped a blue pill into a glass beaker. It immediately burst into a rush of bubbles racing to the top of the water. The man dabbed the sweat off his forehead and offered a tentative smile. "It works as soon as it hits the liquid, sir."

A deep scowl crossed the taller man's thin face. "I can see that, Arnold, and I prefer Sir Charles. Will it do what I want it to?"

Arnold gulped loudly as the water turned a bloody red and boiled with no heat source. Its froth spilled over the beaker like a volcano exploding. "Yes, Sir Charles. The test is going exactly as planned. We will test it in its chocolate form tomorrow. Its reaction will happen in the mouth and stomach, but we are confident it will succeed."

Sir Charles's thick black eyebrows hovered over the bloodshot eyes that defined his madness. "Good, good. I need it to be perfect for Halloween. You understand?"

"Of course, Sir Charles. We will test it tomorrow."

"On the rats, I assume?" His black-clothed body sank into the shadows, but the clinical lighting from the high ceiling shone directly on his displeased face.

Arnold tugged at his itchy white collar. "Yes, it's wise to try it on the animal subjects first because—"

Sir Charles slammed his fist on the white Formica counter. The beaker containing the roaring concoction tipped precariously but stayed upright and held its precious elixir. "This potion is meant for humans, not rats. I can't believe I have to think of everything. I will bring some healthy young specimens from the holding area."

Arnold covered his mouth as bile forced its way up. He pushed it back down, along with his anger. "It might kill the children if the formula isn't right."

"Then kill them, but get it right." The words were spoken with no emotion.

Arnold gulped and wiped away more sweat without responding.

"Arnold, have you found something to alter your mind?" Sir Charles paused.

He shook his head vigorously. He knew the rules. No drinking or taking mind-numbing relief. It would not only take him off the project but cost him and his partner their lives. "No, Sir Charles."

Sir Charles appeared satisfied. "Why do you think I bought a major candy company and spent a small fortune on this lab?"

"For us to do experiments." Arnold looked at his colleagues for support, but they were in the same position—forced help.

Sir Charles put his hands on his hips. "Right, and you are being allowed to continue your pathetic existence. And what do I want these chocolates for?"

Arnold flashed back to grammar school, answering the demanding teacher. "Halloween."

The man sighed loudly. "Sometimes I think you were dropped on your head as a baby. Humans, yourself included, have always ruined my best ideas. The zombies from your experiment will keep the world busy, then I will slip in and take control of everything, understand?"

"Yes, Sir Charles, but no one has stopped you from doing what you want for centuries." The words escaped before he could stop them. A gasp came from behind him.

Sir Charles folded his long arms and bent to be at eye level with Arnold. His breath reminded Arnold of a slaughterhouse, which he was. "They stopped my dear mother when they hammered a stake into her heart. I'll never forget her screams or my rage. It's been simmering inside since that day. Luckily, after I was exiled into the forest, the *real* monster took pity on me and gave me immortality—like I might do for you if you please me."

Arnold held his hands up and briefly dipped his head. "I'm sorry, Sir Charles. I meant no disrespect. You are so powerful already. That's what I meant. Everyone fears you."

Sir Charles patted Arnold on the head, stood straight, and adjusted his black hat. "It took decades to gain that respect in my community. When it was time, I took revenge on the entire town that punished an innocent woman. That's never been enough, however. No, Arnold, not at all. Humans haven't changed over the centuries. They still live and act in fear, so I waited and watched. Now your kind has the technology to give me what I've been imagining—an effervescent potion that makes humans into compliant sleepwalkers—zombies. My creatures will care for those who don't eat the chocolate."

"Aren't you killing your food supply?" Arnold's complexion was pale from being underground for the last few years, but now it took on a shade of green. He saw it reflected in the mirrored camera that watched every move they made.

"My creatures will never deny me their blood, but I admit I like the chase, so leaving some to hunt will be nice. No one can challenge me, though, got that?"

"Yes, Sir Charles."

A smirk filled the sharpness of his youthful face. "Great. Now I'll bring you your test subjects."

Arnold nodded and turned back to his work. He'd had his own

formula ready for a long time and even boldly shared it today instead of what Sir Charles was expecting. This liquid changed the subjects' cells in all the studies, and the rats had survived the last test. He offered his lab partner a weak smile, but Patty turned her tearstained face away from him and the all-seeing mirror. At least she had her husband and three children to share her nights in their private cell. He had the same privilege with his partner and cat, but most of the others were crammed together in small spaces, usually not with family members.

The image of all the tears shed because of this monster made Arnold push aside his years of training and make a rare, rash decision. "I'm done with this. I know our formula will work."

Patty froze as realization crossed her face. "That could fry your brain or worse! Think of David!"

Arnold brought the bubbling concoction to his lips, and a power he hadn't experienced since he was tricked into this nightmare surged through him. He smiled. "It won't, Patty."

"Please wait."

He didn't listen, only dipped his finger in and stirred the potion. The liquid had cooled, and the bubbles had returned. Patty gasped loudly as he gulped it down. Finished, he tossed the beaker into the trash can and burped loudly as the bubbles danced in his stomach.

Patty and the others were backing away from him as Sir Charles entered the lab, tugging two terrified little boys behind him. His shrewd eyes missed nothing. "You poor, pathetic fool. Well, you will be the lab rat now, Arnold."

Arnold's blood rushed the potion to all parts of his body. He knew what came next and steeled himself for it. As he collapsed onto the ground, withering like a thirsty flower under a scorching summer sun, everything went black, but only briefly. Then the light seemed to come from his pores. He jumped up and grinned.

"It appears your junk doesn't work, Arnold. Either you get it right within twenty-four hours, or you, David, and that horrible cat die.

Put these things in a cage so they don't run away and cause a mess." He pushed the crying children toward Patty.

Arnold embraced a strength and power like those of a cartoon superhero. It had taken him three years to create the formula, but now he was a perfect monster killer. Arnold and Patty had secretly stimulated a part of the brain untapped by humanity while working on the required formula to repress the mind. He stepped before Sir Charles with a huge grin while Patty comforted the little boys.

"Don't come any closer, Arnold. I'm only going to warn you once." Sir Charles's bravado deflated as Arnold reached out to the pale bloodsucker and pushed past him.

Before Sir Charles could respond, Arnold broke their tormentor's neck, ripped his head off, and carelessly tossed it aside. As the blood-less head rolled away, Arnold swore it asked why. He learned all he needed to know from that vile creature's final thoughts. Everything they had been told over the last three years in captivity had been a lie, including the reward of eternal life. They were less than a herd of cows to Sir Charles, and to be ended by them was a tremendous humiliation.

The images Arnold witnessed from the monster's mind were so clear. He saw a woman with a wooden stake in her chest burning in bright orange flames. That had to be Sir Charles's mother. There were many terrified faces as they took their last breath, all jumbled together, but the last lucid thought was a picture of flames that consumed everything. Arnold shook his head. That must have been when he took down an entire village to avenge his mother. That young boy had become what the villagers first claimed his mother was—a deranged monster.

Following a round of congratulations, Arnold released everyone and led the way to freedom. He ripped open the steel door that had confined 231 people. They slowly made their way through the tunnel to the surface, where the door opened easily into a nightmare.

The landscape was charred and bare. There was nothing for miles. His newly gained powers reached out and found nothing alive except for what had survived in the ocean. He calculated the chemicals in the environment. Though charred, it was safe for them to live.

Being imprisoned by a crazy vampire had saved them from their own kind. Humanity had finally crossed the line and set up a conflict that killed everyone but them and the animals still below that were kept for experiments or food. It wasn't getting revenge for his mother's death that had been Sir Charles's last thought but the world's demise. The vampire wanted control of those he held hostage so he could recreate the world in his distorted image.

Arnold's tears flowed as he held David and the ground released a sulfuric effervescent reminder of what fear and hate can produce. This small group had become the survivors, passengers of the new Noah's ark. It would be up to them to start over. He hoped this time they would do it right.

The Bonsai

For Danielle

THE FOG SLOWLY CREPT IN, covering the landscape in a soft, gray blanket. The distant lighthouse's mournful cry warned the ships of land. The gentle ocean sway had always been my meditation, but the sound grated on my nerves today.

I turned my attention to the bonsai that Henry had named Blossom. It had been a wedding gift from Henry's parents. Blossom had lived at the edge of the cliff for over forty years. Here is where I scattered Henry's ashes last week. Sitting on the bench made of driftwood that Henry made right after retiring three years ago didn't bring me the closure I desired.

Our golden years were cut short by aggressive cancer. I was left with an empty ocean-view house and Blossom. She was the closest we came to kids since I could only miscarry babies, not have them. After losing three, we couldn't bear any more losses. We let our dream go. We became each other's everything, and now I was lost without his serene smile and quick wit.

Dr. Denny's declaration rang hollow this morning. "You're in perfect health, Mrs. Duffy. You'll live to be a hundred years old."

I had smiled, but inside I wished it had been bad news. How could I live for thirty more years without the one person who made life worth living?

A sudden chill ran through me, and I pulled my knitted cap down over my ears and zipped my coat higher.

"I should have brought my scarf today, Henry."

A lone gull dove past me, screeching toward the open water. The cold filled me, and I pushed off the bench. "Henry?"

I scanned the area. Nothing. I shook my head as a gust of wind tore the hat off.

"Hey!" I chased my blue hat as it headed for the cliff. "Come back here!"

My foot slipped on a rock, and I slid helplessly toward the edge. My only hope was grabbing Blossom. I had one chance, or I'd be painfully joining Henry. My hand reached and missed the tree, and my foot was off the cliff. Everything moved in slow motion as I prayed for a miracle.

Blossom bent toward me, and I swear her branches were reaching for me like hands as a massive blast of wind blew in from the ocean. A branch tightly encircled my arm and prevented certain death. I hugged the tree as tears ran down my face.

Carefully I moved my fingers and then the rest of my body. Nothing was broken, just bruised. I lay there for a moment, taking deep breaths to calm my racing heart.

"No one would believe what just happened, Henry."

Black tennis shoes were suddenly next to Blossom.

"I believe you, Darcie." The familiar voice soothed me.

I sat up so quickly I hit my head on the bottom branch.

"Careful, sweetheart. I wish I could help you up."

I rubbed my head, where a bump was already forming. "I either have brain damage or I'm dead."

The loud laughter that I so loved drowned out the ocean. "Neither."

I moved a branch and was greeted by the man I loved, who was now in his thirties. "But you're dead. How can I see you?"

He shook his head. That brown curl I had loved to play with bounced around his ear. "In my panic to stop you from going over the cliff, I communicated with Blossom. She offered her life to the wind to save you."

The once beautiful tree was split down the middle. The jagged wood bit into my hands as I grasped it. Ignoring the minor cuts, I flipped over onto my knees. Then, using it like a crooked cane, I pulled myself to standing with a loud grunt. I was eye to eye with Henry. It was unnerving—I could see through those beautiful eyes. "Blossom?"

"Yes. I didn't know that was possible, but I'm grateful to her. I wish it could have been me saving you, but I didn't know how. She did. Wise tree."

I shook my head. "I don't understand. How can you bargain with the wind?"

Henry gestured to the landscape. "The wind and the world are alive where I am. Anything is possible. Blossom is with me, using the last of her strength to help me talk to you."

"I'm so confused. Is our tree a spirit? Can I see her?"

"Yes, a spirit, but too weak right now to appear to you. She wants you to know she's eager to play with our children."

I caught my breath. "Our children are there?"

He held out his arms. "Of course—they have always stayed close to us."

"This is crazy."

His face softened, and he reached out. All I could feel was the cold, not his warm touch. "As much as I want you here with me, I know you still have so much good left to do. I love you."

"I love you too."

The bench behind was more in focus now. He was fading away.

"Blossom says you'll soon find what you're meant to do next, and you'll plant another bonsai next to her. Its soul will watch over you. Bye, sweetheart."

"You can't leave."

"I can't stay. Be happy."

"Wait!"

Then he was gone. I dragged myself to the bench, collapsed onto it, and let the tears flow. The wind kicked up, finishing the destruction of the bonsai. I slowly made my way back to the house. As I climbed the stairs, I noticed a tiny gray kitten crying by the red door. I scooped it up.

As soon as the kitten was settled in a warm box, I went back to look for the mother and the rest of the kittens. I have yet to find them. This was what Henry was talking about—my love of animals. I always wanted to have them and care for injured ones, but Henry's severe allergies prevented that.

I could volunteer at our local wildlife rehabilitation center or foster unwanted pets. First, though, I had a little guy to care for. He had a home with me. He was purring contentedly in his warm blanket after gobbling down some tuna. Maybe I could start an animal sanctuary. Thanks to Blossom's sacrifice and Henry's love, there were many possibilities. I wouldn't let them down!

Stranded

A novelette based on *An Unusual Island*
Dedicated to our inner child

Shipwrecked on a tropical island, I've never been more full of joy. This feeling has been a rarity lately. You see, I did everything that was expected of me in life. I got married, raised kids, worked hard, cared for my parents until they died, and paid the bills on time. I lived the so-called American dream and couldn't complain, but something was missing. When my husband and I retired, we finally had extra time to do everything we wanted.

It hurt that the kids and grandkids were always too busy to include us in their distant lives, but we found things to do. We gardened, watched movies, visited national parks, and even saw a whale breach off the Pacific Coast. All those things we never had time for when raising our kids were now checked off our list. Yes, we were lucky we had a full life and were still healthy, but each day became the same. It was like we were sitting around waiting to die as comfortably as possible. Let's say I wasn't in a positive place.

One afternoon we watched an old *Twilight Zone* episode where older people got a second chance at life by playing kick-the-can. I asked Rob, "What is our kick-the-can?"

I got the expected and usually appreciated response. "You will always be my kick-the-can, Gigi."

But the question got me wondering when my gaze settled on a picture of us smiling against a Hawaiian sunset. It was where we honeymooned, and we went back thirty years later for our second honeymoon. We even talked about moving there but decided we'd be too far from our family—a twelve-hour flight instead of a six-hour one. We'd seen all the islands, but there was one thing we always joked about doing. Rent a boat and experience the islands from a new perspective.

For the first time in a while, there was that spark inside. Something new.

My husband fought the idea. "Honey, we aren't as young as we used to be. And think of the cost. We need our savings in case something happens to one of us."

"This trip won't break us, and we could cut back on other things. Please, this is something I need." I gave him the wide-eyed look he had never denied.

After our physicals, the doctor declared us healthy for our post-working age. We were deemed able to embark on an adventure. I gathered details that included the flight, food, and boat rental. In my mind, it didn't differ from staying in an excellent hotel, which I was a fan of, but after retirement, we avoided that extra expense. Soon I became discouraged, finding most rentals way out of our price range, until a new ad popped up from a private owner at a price we could afford. I quickly contacted him, keeping in mind that it could be a scam.

"Hello," a promising older man answered.

I cleared my throat. "Hi, I'm calling about your boat rental in Hawaii."

"Wow. I just placed the ad. Who am I talking to?"

I hesitated. Could I trust him? His voice sounded so familiar, but who did I know in Hawaii? "Gigi Thurmond."

There was a deep intake of breath. "Gigi? This is Bart Collins. This isn't Gigi that went to Bellmont High School, is it?"

"Yes, it is! I can't believe it. You live in Hawaii now?"

We quickly caught up. He had dated my best friend from high school. We all hung out together until everyone went their way after graduation. We sent each other Christmas cards for years but hadn't talked since we retired. How lucky was it that an old friend had a boat to rent? I booked the boat, confident I could convince Rob, who had been in the navy for four years and had experience.

"My only requirement is you sit through an old guy's boring tutorial after you go online and get your boater educational card."

"Knowing you, Bart, I highly doubt it will be boring."

Before I knew it, we were at the Ala Wai Boat Harbor in Honolulu on a thirty-five-foot white boat called *Nina*, getting what turned out to be a rather dull and detailed three-day boat lesson from Bart and his wife, Nina. After promising a dinner together when we returned, we set sail with comprehensive maps of where to go and what to do if the meteorological conditions changed. The weather and winds were calm. We had plenty of food and adventure in our hearts. I was in charge of the marine radio, the galley, the cabin, and the weather. We would back each other up during our eight-week excursion.

I pointed to the darkening horizon. "Looks like a storm is coming, but the weather service forecasts sunny skies!"

"Maybe it isn't headed our way. But if they're wrong, we're close enough to Kauai to take shelter if needed." Rob frowned at the clouds.

Angry waves pounded us before we got near any island. We were being tossed around like an old baseball. My gut clenched with each wave's impact.

Rob clutched the polished wooden helm. His knuckles were as pale as I knew my face was. He planted his feet and pointed but still hung on to the boat's helm, which seemed to have a mind of its own.

"Kauai should be right there. The instruments must be acting up because of the storm." Rob shook his head as I sank into the blue couch.

I wasn't sure how he kept on his feet. It was like being on a roller coaster. He captained our small ship bravely. I had never been more proud of him.

A chill shot through me as the boat shuddered. I wrapped an old gray wool blanket around my sunburned shoulders. "Rob! This feels like we're in the middle of a hurricane."

"It does." His expression was grim. "Put on your life jacket, honey. It's gonna be a bumpy ride."

I tugged it on and pulled myself from the couch to stand by his side. *We were going to die together, at least.* An immense wave crashed across the bow as if the storm had read my mind. Everything went black.

I awoke with the sun shining brightly through a porthole.

"Rob!" I cried, reaching for him. "Are you okay?"

He gently squeezed my hand, rolled his shoulders, and stretched his legs. "Not a scratch. What about you?"

I tentatively moved around. "I'm fine."

He nodded and pulled himself up with a grunt. "I don't think *Nina* is okay."

He was right. Bart's boat was on its side on a black sandy beach. We carefully stepped over the clothes and supplies littered across the disassembled cabin and climbed out the door.

I gasped. "We're lucky to be alive!"

Rob pointed to the boat. "That hole is as big as me. I'm going to check if the radio works."

Neither the radio nor our cell phones worked, so we spent the rest of the day pulling out blankets and pillows to camp on the beach under a star-filled sky. After a dinner of sandwiches and chips, we both fell into an exhausted sleep serenaded by the gentle ocean waves.

The morning sun finally pried open my eyes. I reached for Rob and found a discarded blanket. No surprise, as he was a morning person. I yawned and stretched, expecting everything to hurt. Nothing did. Still blurry-eyed, I shook the sand from my hair and found a roll of toilet paper next to the crackling fire. I found a private tree to use. When I stepped out, I finally took in the pristine beach that looked like something out of a travel guide.

"Breakfast." Rob handed me a bagel with peanut butter and a French-pressed cup of coffee. The coffee's earthy aroma soothed me. I was glad for his early morning habits—I wasn't productive before noon.

I grinned at him. "Thank you. We should look around and see if anyone is nearby to help us. I'll throw some lunch together."

"You read my mind. I'll find the old compass and gun, just in case." Rob disappeared back into the boat.

Famished, I washed down the sticky bagel with the strong coffee. Feeling more alert, I joined Rob on our shipwreck. With the boat more on its side than upright, it made walking a challenge, and dropping through the door was something more suited to my youthful days.

"Rob?"

"Out here. Be careful in there."

I grinned. "Always."

Things were strewn everywhere like small kids had taken apart a room, but I quickly found a pair of hiking shorts, a turtle tank top, and walking sandals to change into. I dragged a brush through my unruly, tinted red hair and found my toothbrush and floss. I was ready for whatever the day brought in this beautiful paradise that had saved us from certain death.

"The rubber raft is fine if we need to leave, but maybe we should look around first, don't you think?" Rob called from the stern. He was wearing his beige hiking shorts with all the pockets and his Indiana Jones hat.

I sprayed on some sunscreen. "I'd rather stay on solid ground right now."

He walked into the cabin. "Me too. Who knows how long we'd float with no one finding us? The radio and the EPIRB were both destroyed. We can't communicate."

"The EP . . . what?" I found my green backpack and added some bottles of water.

"Emergency position indicating radio beacon. It sends out a signal to let authorities know where we are. I imagine you tuned out that part of our boat lessons." Rob gave me his brightest smile, which didn't reach his deep-blue eyes.

I matched it with the same forced intensity. "Yeah, I probably did. I forgot how much Bart can talk."

Rob shook his head. "He has the gift of gab. You ready to explore?"

"I sure am. Let me finish packing our food."

"Can I help?"

"I got it. You should put some sunscreen on, though."

Soon we were enmeshed in a beautiful, lush tropical forest of interesting dimensions. I was as energized as the plants had to be to grow this size. "Isn't this remarkable?"

"It is," Rob agreed. He pointed to a group of large red flowers. "Never seen anything like it. One flower would cover our entire living room and outscent your roses."

I winked. "It would. It reminds me of that show that was on when we were kids. You know where they landed on a planet and everyone and everything was huge?"

"*Land of the Giants*? Yeah, it does, but I think we're still on Earth. Too bad about the boat, though. Glad Bart said they had it fully insured." Rob frowned.

I patted his shoulder. "I'm sure he'll get a brand-new boat out of it. I doubt even the most experienced captain would have avoided damage in that storm. We were lucky."

Rob grabbed my hand, squeezed it, and smiled gently. "Every *thing* can be replaced, but *you* can't. That's all I care about right now."

"Ditto," I replied, adding, "We can't worry about the damage or insurance right now because we have an island to explore, Mr. Thurmond."

Rob grinned. "That we do, Mrs. Thurmond."

I couldn't absorb all the beauty. It was overwhelming, as if I were looking at the world through a young child's eyes. "I honestly wouldn't mind if they never found us. This is so gorgeous, and that word doesn't do it justice." I let out a contented sigh and shifted my feet to get around a black volcanic rock.

"I wouldn't mind that either." Rob smiled with a glance at my arthritic foot. It had been aching since I broke it a few years back. "We have some painkillers in the boat, but I didn't think to bring some with us."

"No, for once, I'm in no pain. That was a happy sigh."

We spent the next few hours hiking around, not finding another living being on our way or any signs of people having been there besides us. We turned around a corner and found a pristine waterfall.

"Come on!" I dropped his hand and did something I hadn't done in years, run in pure abandon through bright yellow wildflowers to the clearest pond I'd ever seen. The massive hole in our boat was forgotten as I kicked off my sandals and dipped my feet into the cool waters.

Rob dunked a finger in the water, tasted it, and spit it out. "This is freshwater, Gigi. We can boil it. With water, coconuts, and fish, we should be okay. I have a talent for fishing, you know."

I stepped into the water up to my knees. "Yes, you've told me, but I still hold the record for the biggest fish caught."

He pulled off his hiking shoes, came up behind me in the water, and wrapped his arms around me. "For now you do, Mrs. Thurmond."

I repressed a smile. "We'll see." I pointed to a grove of bushes with massive purple berries. "Those look like blueberries. We should try one."

"If I saw an animal eating one, we'd know they *might* be okay, but . . . Do you see that fish there? I'm willing to drink this water, but strange plants? Let's wait. We'll be okay. I'm sure we'll be rescued soon, even if we don't want to be." Rob grinned and kissed my cheek.

I leaned on his familiar broad shoulder. "Right, but if, at some point, I'm starving to death, I'm eating one."

"Deal."

I splashed Rob and giggled. "We should have a picnic here."

"Yes, that's a great idea, " Rob said with a distant smile. His gaze was fixed on the tree line.

I scanned the area that was holding his attention. Something small darted through the vines and trees. Small branches cracked, tracking its movement.

"What was that?" I asked.

"Um, maybe a deer or whatever they have on these islands like that."

I shook my head. "What if it's a boar?"

Rob shrugged. "Well, we'd have a food supply, and I have my gun, but I'd rather stick to fish. Anyway, it's gone now. First live thing we've seen except the fish. No birds, insects, or anything. An unusual island we crashed on."

"I don't mind having an unusual island all to ourselves. Besides, I think this is what we needed."

Rob grinned at me, making him look thirty years old again with his handsome, chiseled face, sparkly azure eyes, and a mop of gray hair that had replaced the brown years ago. He wasn't one of those men who lost hair on the head and gained it back in their ears, nostrils, and eyebrows. Maybe he had put on a few extra pounds, but so had I. There was a familiar attraction coursing through me that I hadn't experienced in a couple of years. I smiled back.

Rob put his arm around me. "I completely agree, Gigi. This is exactly what we needed."

A picture of our home life flashed through my mind, dampening my mood. "Yes, things have been weird with family and stuff back home."

Rob gently stroked my cheek and held my gaze. "True, but we've never been the problem, just the world. Our kids have their own lives."

"They do, but they didn't have to do it the way they did." I offered a half frown.

Rob grabbed my hand and squeezed it. "They didn't get lucky like us."

"We can only hope they find what they're looking for. I love them, but their daily drama is draining. Carter loves the single life and is still searching for himself, which he hasn't found in a bar. Then our little Sasha has a husband who's determined to become the richest man in Florida. Not sure how he stays out of jail with his business practices. Their idea of happiness is sure different from ours." I shrugged.

"Yes, I agree. I miss the grandkids, but they're teenagers now and not interested in hanging out with Grandma and Grandpa when we visit them in Palm Beach. Carter doesn't want kids, so that leaves us."

I smiled. "I have an idea. When we get home, I vote we sell the house and settle down on a houseboat in Oregon. Remember, we always talked about it before we had kids? A much better plan than sitting around waiting to die like we've been doing."

Rob grinned. "I remember that. I second this idea."

After a peaceful meal by a waterfall, we made love. Not in the usual weekend way, but with youthful lust and passion. We were both breathless as I snuggled up next to my husband of forty-five years on the soft green grass. We fell asleep wearing nothing but a smile, listening to the sound of water cascading down the rocky cliff. I only woke up when the chill of the setting sun alerted us to the approaching nightfall.

Rob jumped into the pond, and I joined him. After another passionate interlude, we finally got dressed. We held hands like we did when we first started dating, which was good because my body might have floated away in a bubble of happiness. Being shipwrecked was the best thing that had happened to us in a long time. Nothing could kill my high.

Pushing through the trees to the beach, we found a surprise awaiting us.

Flames shot up from our firepit. "Um, do you think the fire restarted from this morning?" I glanced at Rob.

Rob shook his head and crossed his arms over his chest. "It could happen, I suppose, but highly unlikely. It was out when I tried to heat more water for coffee."

"Maybe the wind stirred it up, and a log rolled into it. Otherwise, I've got nothing."

Rob scanned the area. "Let's check it out, but we need to be careful. Something doesn't feel right, Gigi."

Hand in hand, we scoured the area and the boat. Nothing.

"I guess it relit. I'll gather up some stuff for dinner. We'd better finish the perishables tonight."

Rob checked his gun and put it back into his waistband. That sent a chill through me. "Sure, good idea. Let me help you."

It took us a while to gather all that was needed in the mess, but soon we were carrying down our food in the pots and pans. Two bowls of beans were waiting for us when we got to the fire, and an empty can of chili was tossed to the side.

"Someone is here," I stated the obvious.

"Yes, and while we were inside the boat." Rob pulled out his gun, examining the horizon.

"What is going on, Rob? Is someone playing a joke on us?"

"I don't know, but at least we know we aren't alone." Rob rubbed his temples with his free hand.

I threw up my hands. "They can't expect us to eat this."

He examined the bowls. "Right, we aren't going to eat chili from the can served by an unknown chef. We have our own food to cook. I'll stand guard if you don't mind cooking. Unless you'd feel better in the boat? We could eat the food out of the cans."

Rob pushed the bowls away from the fire with his foot.

"No, I want to use this food, and you have your weapon. Besides, if they wanted to hurt us, they could have already, right?" I asked, more hopeful than I was.

"Yes, but they're observing us. We sleep on the boat tonight, where there's a door to close and lock. I know it's sideways, but we can make it work. Tomorrow we'll figure this out."

Goosebumps covered my arms as I nodded. Had they been watching us all day? Then they got quite a show. My face reddened as I cooked the hamburger and boiled the pasta. I couldn't even say out loud what they might have witnessed.

Rob paced around the area. "I don't see any footprints, but I'd feel better if we were inside. You almost done?"

"I have to drain the pasta, but I can add the sauce inside."

"I'll carry that," Rob reached out for the pasta.

"I can carry it and the other pan. You make sure we get to the boat safely." He gently kissed the top of my head and followed me into the boat. The meal was eaten quietly, with Rob checking the windows.

We fell into an uneasy sleep in the broken boat. Every sound was suspicious, but the ocean breeze and distant buzzing lulled us into slumber.

A crash startled me awake in the darkness. Rob groaned and turned over after I shook him. I carefully stepped over him and peeked out the porthole that was now a skylight. I gasped at what I saw around the roaring fire.

Upright reptilian creatures that appeared humanlike in their movements. They didn't wear shoes on their wide, bare feet, but they were dressed in a kind of dark uniform. Their arms were shaped like ours, but their skin was shiny like a snake's. There was no hair on their sunset-colored heads, and enormous eyes were widely set over a small, square nose. There were holes where the ears should be. They were almost pretty, but their wide mouths concerned me. When they opened them, large, pointed teeth appeared. That made me wonder what was on their menu and why they were cooking and cleaning up after us. Were we an ingredient?

This has to be a dream. I pinched my arm and felt the pain. Not. A. Dream. I was frozen, watching them clean up the plates and sweep around the fire. There were five of them. One pointed to our boat. I ducked away from the skylight when a loud, high-pitched buzzing filled my ears. My body was heavy. I wanted to wake Rob but couldn't as I sank to the ground. Before I knew it, I was curled on the floor, and it was morning. I shook Rob awake and launched into the story of the night before.

"Reptile people?" Rob asked. "That was quite a dream if it even got you to sleepwalk and sleep on the floor. That must have been hard on your back."

"It wasn't a dream, and my back is fine, thanks," I countered, not mentioning my doubts.

Rob held his hands up. "Okay, okay. I thought . . . You don't play jokes, but you must admit this sounds crazy, and I know you aren't. What if I was telling you this story? How would you respond?"

"I would believe you, of course." I couldn't make eye contact because I wouldn't have believed him.

"Of course you would." Rob's voice was laced with sarcasm.

"I would," I protested weakly.

"Well, let's spend the day looking for these, um, reptile people. I have my gun, and you should carry a knife so we don't become an entrée."

"Funny. But if you saw them, you'd understand," I mumbled, opening a drawer and grabbing the biggest knife I could find.

"I will accept that what you witnessed last night was real. But they didn't bother us, only cleaned up. We didn't see them while we looked around the island. I will assume they won't attack us, but we don't know what they are. That buzzing sound seems to affect us, though, and I think we could counter that with the earplugs you brought." Rob grinned. His years of being married meant he would play along.

I sighed and pulled open the drawer I thought I'd put the plugs in. The drawer fell off its track, and scissors, tape, and the rest of its contents came crashing down, narrowly missing my foot.

"You okay, Gigi?"

"Yup, nothing broke this time, and I found them." I held up the orange foam plugs.

Rob grinned. "Well, that's good. I wonder . . . "

"Wonder what?" I stuffed a backpack with protein bars, cheese, berries, nuts, chips, and cookies.

"I wonder if a group of kids live nearby and dressed up in costumes to play a joke on the old people."

"We haven't seen any houses, but that doesn't mean anything. But what if it isn't a costume and we're part of some weird government experiment?"

Rob shrugged as he grabbed the bagels and peanut butter. The conversation was getting weird, and we needed to eat.

We spent the day exploring the jungle and then the island's coast. There was nothing. We had another picnic by another amazing waterfall. Then my mind hijacked our moment. As the water cascaded down the rocks, I thought about all the spoiled food that would have to be thrown away. I thought about the knife next to me as I dipped my feet in the cool water and those reptilian people as the fragrant scent of the flowers filled my soul. I thought about our abundance of canned food while we made love. Afterward, Rob kept watching the surrounding trees. Still, we had each other to face whatever this island brought us.

I wasn't comfortable drying naked in the sun and quickly got dressed and finger-combed my hair. Soon we were on our way. We stayed on the island's outer edge, hoping to circle back to camp, but it kept going and going.

"We should head back. Tomorrow we can go in the other direction," I suggested. I downed the rest of my water.

We got lost several times heading back, passing by the same berry bush at least three times. The landscape tricked us into the same route, although I didn't know how. Finally, when the sun was setting, we came to the clearing where our boat was and found another fire roaring. They didn't leave us food this time, but my body was still covered in goosebumps as I tightly gripped my knife.

We bypassed the fire and quickly headed into the boat. After we heated some minestrone on the propane camping stove, we climbed into our makeshift bed.

"Could you warm water for me? I think I'll need some coffee if we're going to pull an all-nighter."

"Sure." Rob clicked on the small propane burner and double-checked the door to the deck. It had been broken in half, but he had repaired it with a board. Good thing the boat was fully equipped.

Coffee kept me awake as we closed our eyes. I pretended to be asleep in my sweat suit. I didn't know if that was required for a visit, but I thought we should repeat last night's process. The buzzing zapped my ears, so I inserted the plugs. Rob was already asleep.

"Rob," I gently whispered and then placed the plugs in his ears.

His eyes popped open, and he looked around. I shook my head and placed a finger on my lips as we lay there for what seemed to be forever before I peeked. Nothing. The minutes stretched into an hour as Rob grasped my hand. He nodded to what used to be the skylight but was now our window. We slowly got up and settled into our chairs, watching. Finally, lights began flickering outside. Rob was asleep again. I gave him a gentle nudge.

I smugly pointed, and Rob slowly moved to my side. His mouth dropped open as mine had. Reptile people. It sure didn't look like costumes to me. Now to figure out what they wanted and where we were. I pointed to the door and attempted to stand, but Rob grabbed my arm, tugging me back next to him. The movement jarred the boat, causing a creak. I gulped. Their lights went out, and they retreated into the trees. I took a plug out and heard a loud buzzing. I yawned and replaced it.

"The door," I mouthed and pointed.

We made our way quietly through the scattered mess to the door.

"Let's see if they left anything behind." Rob slowly turned the doorknob with one hand, his gun in the other.

The door creaked, protesting its angled position. It sounded louder than ever. We were met with empty darkness until a reptile person stepped out from behind the open door. Rob tried to pull me back and slam the door, but it was too late. The creature inserted its foot in the door, grabbed Rob's gun, and tossed it away. Then it held its hands up as Rob pushed me behind him and grabbed the broom.

The creature towered over us. It was clothed in fitted black pants and a baggy sleeveless shirt instead of the black uniform I'd seen the night before. It looked less imposing in more casual dress. Still, there was its sheer size. It could knock us out easily or even break our necks, and there would be nothing we could do about it. Large brown eyes were rimmed with feathery black lashes that flashed a kindness lacking in the muffled baritone voice that penetrated my earplugs. It pointed to my ears and then outward. I glanced at Rob, who pulled one plug out. Cautiously I copied him.

"We aren't here to hurt you, but you are in danger. If you want your gun back, you can have it later, I promise. We were going to move you tonight while you slept and explain everything in the morning, but you stayed awake."

"We are going nowhere with you, and I would like our gun back now." Rob stood a little taller and firmed his shoulders.

"I wish we had more time, but another ship crashed with yours. They found your boat this evening. They want your supplies and will take them and whatever else they want." The creature's dark gaze rested on me.

"We'll take our chances, thank you," Rob replied. "Now, if you will kindly move your foot."

My questions were stuck in my throat. Up close it looked almost human, except for the scales and holes for ears.

It blinked several times and looked back. A loud sigh followed. "They're nearly here. Sorry." A loud sound vibrated through my body, and the next thing I knew, I was waking up in a bed next to

Rob, who was snoring loudly. We weren't on the boat. We were in an unfamiliar sterile room with no door.

I hopped out of the feather-soft bed in my pink sweats with the urge to run screaming out of there, but what would I be running to? A change of clothes for each of us was neatly folded on a white cushioned chair next to the bed, and our sandals were under them on a floor that resembled an abalone shell. I cautiously peeked outside the door. No reptile people were lurking in the long, creamy-white hall. The floor was the same as in our room, and it was breathtaking under the soft blue lights that made it sparkle, but I didn't have time to admire it. I quickly dressed and shook Rob awake.

"I had the strangest dream." Rob pulled the covers over his head.

I shook him more urgently. "It wasn't a dream, Rob. Wake up. I don't know where we are."

Rob shot up, looking around. "I, um . . . "

I held back an eye roll. "Right. There are your clothes."

Rob didn't respond as he dressed faster than he had in years. He grabbed my hand as we crept out the door.

"I need to use the girls' room." I glanced back at the only door the room had.

"Now?"

"Yes."

Sure enough, the door led to a massive bathroom with the biggest shower I'd ever seen. I peeked into the toilet, and it appeared okay. They used things as we did. I didn't know whether that made me feel safe or terrified. I splashed water on my face and rinsed my mouth. Rob quickly followed me, and soon we were back in the hall. We didn't get far before we met the same reptile person.

It extended a hand. "I hope you were comfortable. I want to welcome you to my home."

Rob studied it without taking the offered scaly hand or replying.

It moved its hand back down by its side in an awkward motion. "You must understand you aren't prisoners here but guests. We needed to protect you."

A frown passed over Rob's face as he entered his lawyer mode of faked confidence. "Well, I could argue that bringing us here without our consent makes us unwilling guests, at the very least. I respectfully request you tell us where we are, whom we need protection from, and your intentions." Rob put his arm tightly around my shoulder.

"Yes, I can honor your request. You are next to Earth, and another group of humans means you harm. Our only intention was to help you. I know this must be confusing to you." It paused and glanced at something that looked like a smartwatch. It was reading something.

"Confusing is an understatement." Rob's grip tightened, and I flinched. He quickly loosened his grasp and mouthed "sorry" to me.

A whiff of flowers, like jasmine on a hot summer's day but sweeter, hit my nose. A calm wave flowed through my taut body while my racing heart slowed down to normal. Rob's hold on my shoulders became a massage. "Can you explain what 'next to Earth' means and what harm is expected?" I asked.

The reptile person smiled, showing teeth that looked even more terrifying up close. "We aren't *on* Earth but floating in your ocean in our dimension. The other humans, full of malice, came to our dimension with you in the storm. They had already been here because a true storm pushed them here. It happens sometimes. We created a storm to send them back into your world. Unfortunately, when they spotted you, they decided to be like . . . pirates, I believe you call them. We summed up their character quickly when they were here. Their hearts were full of greed and cruelty. The things they bragged about to each other—well, I won't repeat them. We couldn't be responsible for them robbing and hurting you, so we pulled you into our world to keep you safe. The problem with that was those pirates got sucked back here with you. We've had difficulty keeping you separate on opposite sides of the island." A loud beep came from the communicator. "Hang on a moment. I have to answer this."

"No problem." Rob snapped and glanced down at me with a

frown. My weak smile tried to ease his protective displeasure about our situation.

The reptile bunched its hairless eyebrows together and punched something into its communicator. When it looked up, it appeared satisfied. "Sorry. That needed my response. I can see you are upset with my explanation, and I don't blame you. We are fully responsible for your predicament and offer our apologies. Maybe a bit of our history will ease your mind. My people are from a planet much like Earth. We became the dominant species, like you. Our society had many issues that led to an intense war that my side won. The aftermath proved deadly to every living being on our planet. This was when the Elders came. We left our planet until it can recover. You can compare this amazing ship and our animals to Noah and his ark. I know it's a lot to take in, but the Elders watch over all of us, and we aren't the only ones in the surrounding dimensions with the ability to create storms to return wayward humans. There is a society of bird people who have a similar ship nearby. Although there's no communication with other worlds, with a few exceptions like you."

"Another dimension and bird people? I feel like I'm in one of those bad sci-fi movies from the fifties. This is . . . I don't even know what to say," Rob admitted as he rubbed his head.

"I can imagine. We were surprised when the Elders appeared and gathered two of each of our strongest animals, birds, and fish. Then they picked through our survivors, looking for the purest of hearts. They wisely left families intact and offered a second chance. Only a couple turned down the offer. Then they used a storm to get us off our planet. As I mentioned, that's how we travel between dimensions, with this ship programmed to come here."

"So, um . . . I'm afraid I don't know your name?" Rob frowned.

"I'm sorry. The urgency of the situation has eliminated my good manners. My name is . . . in your English language, is Tim." He held out his hand again.

This time, Rob took it. "I am Rob, and this is my wife, Gigi." A look of surprise passed over Rob's face as he released Tim's hand.

I held out my hand, and Tim grasped it. I almost gasped at its warmth. He wasn't cold-blooded as I thought he would be, nor did he feel like a snake. He felt human. I forced a smile and a hello.

Tim nodded as he patted my hand and then let it go. "We knew your names already, but I am happy to exchange them formally."

Rob straightened up, keeping a hand on my shoulder. "Yes, well, I hope you don't mind me speaking for both of us, Gigi?" I shook my head. "We will hold back judgment until we know more. Let me make sure I completely understand what you're telling me. Some Elder beings came from an unknown place and whisked you off a dying planet to hang out near Earth with your animals on a ship that looks like an island?" Rob was back using his court voice again.

"Yes, that happened. These Elder beings aren't like any of us. They are more liquid in appearance, but rocks can hold their energy. The Elders have great power and wisdom throughout this galaxy and the whole universe. They watch over all of us, including your planet, which isn't much better off than ours—and that's why we're here. It's the next place to watch. We have their blessing to speak to you." Tim paused and sighed.

I let out a long exhale as the words exploded in my head like popcorn in an air popper. There was no room left for me to create any recognizable response.

Thankfully, Rob was in excellent form. "So liquid-like Elders will come to Earth at some point and put the chosen few on a ship like yours? Is that what you're saying?"

"That is what I'm saying. If they need to," Tim confirmed with a smile. Long, pointy teeth glimmered in the dim blue lights. I gulped, unable to pull my gaze from them.

"I would like to go home now." My voice was barely above a whisper.

Tim continued smiling with alligator teeth. "We will honor your wish once we get the other humans back to Earth before they kill any more animal guests. Our animals can't be replaced, and mates are left alone to grieve. They tore apart your boat to get parts and anything of value for themselves. So you are our guests until we can replace your boat and get you back to your earthly life."

Rob raised an eyebrow and crossed his arms. "How do we know you'll let us leave? We know about you."

Tim glanced down at his communicator. "Yes, but we will ensure you won't remember us when you leave, so there's no problem. Maybe if I showed you our animals, you'd understand better. Some are like your own, including your extinct dinosaurs. Ours didn't go extinct like yours, but they are leaf eaters like us—well, most of them are. They are fairly common across the galaxy."

"Dinosaurs, really?" Rob asked with a familiar gleam in his eye. He uncrossed his arms and leaned in. That was the magic word for him. He loved dinos. I can't say how many times we've watched *Jurassic Park*.

Tim tilted his head. "Yes. Do they interest you?"

"They do. I did a minor in paleontology. I didn't see much money in it, so I became a family lawyer," Rob admitted with a small shrug.

"Yes, I've learned about your educational and justice systems. Very different from where I come from, where training to fight was more important than education. Your system works much better than ours, but greed always pops up, doesn't it?" Tim held my gaze. His eyes didn't blink. When I finally had to blink, he looked away.

"Yes, but I believe in our systems and the good in people. I feel like justice is usually served." Rob said.

"Yes, of course. It prevents more errors when the criminal gets a trial, but it is faster to execute them on the spot. Don't worry. We left that type of justice behind us. Here, we live for the good of everyone and have had no problems, unlike those bird people. They had an uprising to return to their old ways, and some died. Humans found themselves in the middle of that. Don't worry. The humans were safe, and they were able to help the bird ship in a way that benefited all of us. We got an upgrade to our system. Not that this will mean much to you, but you have my promise that you are safe here, and we always have our eyes on you. We would have preferred sending you back without interaction, but we did what we thought was best. Even if you have breakthrough memories when you leave, I'm not worried. No one would believe you if you told them about us when you returned home." Tim gave us a toothy grin.

"Yeah, they would think we had lost our minds," Rob mumbled.

I took a deep breath, trying to absorb what I was hearing as heat poured off my face. "I feel like I'm losing my mind now. So you were *always* watching us?"

"We provided privacy when needed." Tim fidgeted with his shirt.

"Oh," I looked at Rob, whose bright red cheeks matched my discomfort. I quickly changed the subject. "The other people. Who are they?"

"No idea who they are on Earth, but I imagine they are what you call criminals."

Rob dug his fingers into my skin. I pulled away slightly. He quickly got the hint and relaxed his grip. "Great."

"I think you will enjoy your stay. The length of it is up to you. Your welcome is unlimited." Tim sighed gently, tapping his hands together.

"Unlimited?" Rob glanced at me with his eyebrows pushed together.

"Yes," Tim replied with a hint of impatience as he glared at the red communicator on his wrist. "Decide later, once you've been here a while. Right now, I need to help get rid of our other guests. They aren't cooperating as we'd hoped. We don't want to use force since it's no longer a part of our culture. Don't worry. We will come up with a more passive solution."

"I'm not sure I understand any of this." I shook my head.

Tim tapped on his communicator and looked up with what appeared to be a deep frown. "I understand that. We will talk more later. Breakfast will be brought to you soon. Please wait in your room for your safety until we get them launched. We don't want them to wander in here and hurt you. You are in a kid's room, so there is no door, but your bathroom door locks if it comes to that. I have to go."

Rob's attention was on Tim until he disappeared around the corner. "Sounds like we're prisoners more than guests. How do we even know if there are real people here that want to hurt us? I didn't see anyone else before or after the storm. Did you?"

"No, I didn't," I replied. "What are we going to do?"

"I'm all for adventure and doing new things, but an alien ship? Unbelievable. And dinosaurs? Right. Bird people? I say we are in some sort of weird government experiment. None of this makes sense. The sooner we get out of here and back to our boat, the better. We'll take our chances in the rubber raft on the open sea over this crazy island."

I grabbed Rob's hand tightly and rolled my shoulders. "I agree. This isn't what I had in mind either for adventure. Although I don't think Tim is telling us everything, I kind of believe him."

"You do?"

I nodded.

Rob frowned. "I know I can be closed-minded, but don't you think we should check out our boat and make sure that part is true? Then maybe we could go find these animals he talked about."

"What about the other people here? What if they mean us harm?"

"*If* they're here, they already took what they wanted. We would be stupid to trust what someone who appears to be an alien says to us. Don't you agree?"

I shrugged. "Yes, double-checking facts is logical."

"It is, honey. Let's find a way out of here." Rob tugged on me, and we took off in a run. Each hall looked the same, and we kept running. Oddly, I wasn't breathless when we stopped.

"We're lost." I shook my head.

"Better than being caught. Let's not talk in case someone overhears us." Rob led us in another direction down a long hall.

We kept moving for what seemed like hours but might have been closer to minutes. It was hard to tell. There were no windows, and all the lights were within the walls, giving everything a blue glow.

Finally we entered a vast room with rows of blue stone tables. Gold was interwoven with everything, illuminated by azure crystal lights. The floor was spectacular. It was clear but filled with stones that reminded me of raw rubies, emeralds, opals, sapphires, and diamonds. It was like nothing we had on Earth. Around the tables were heavily padded chairs in blue and green swirl patterns grouped in circles. The far wall was filled with books with unreadable titles. A room like this would cost a fortune on our planet. *Our planet.* That sent a shiver down my body. We dove back into the nearest tunnel and skidded to a halt at a familiar sight.

I threw my hands up. "You're kidding me! This is where we started, Rob! How did we get back to our room?"

Rob's eyes widened as he scanned the tunnel in both directions. "No idea. Everything looks the same."

"There's our promised breakfast. It looks horrible, but the coffee smells good." My mouth watered in anticipation of my morning caffeine.

"No, thanks. It reminds me of split pea soup that has thickened to the point of having to chew it. You know how much I dislike peas. Besides, how can we trust anything, including the coffee they give us?"

"I agree about the food, but you saw the floor in that big room. I've never seen stones like that before in our world."

"Maybe it was manufactured to look alien." Rob shrugged. "Let's try a different direction."

I gave the cup of coffee a parting glance as I inhaled its enticing aroma. We ran in the opposite direction and ended up back in the beautiful, empty, enormous chamber.

We heard a waterfall roar when we tried another set of tunnels. We made our way to the sound but were greeted by a rock wall.

"Now what?" I asked in frustration.

A female-looking reptile person came through the wall. Her eyes widened. "Oh, I thought they had you eating and staying in your room. Can I help you?" She pushed down her long wet shirt over her wet leggings.

"We enjoyed the breakfast, thank you. Tim told us to meet him here after we ate." Rob added a huge grin that matched the width of the Cheshire Cat's.

"Oh, well, I'd stay with you, but I have an important errand and left my communicator back in my room, or I'd let him know you're waiting. I'm Dee, by the way. I know you are Rob and Gigi. Nice to meet you both." She ran off with a quick puzzled glance over her shoulder, and then a burst of air dried her before she turned the corner.

"How did she come through that wall?" I asked, touching it. My hand disappeared into it, and I could feel a cool mist on my fingers.

"Are you okay?" Rob pulled me back.

I held my hand up. "Still attached. This must be like a hologram to hide the exit. Let's find out how big this hole is and get out of here."

"Right out of a sci-fi movie. We better hurry. I bet our new friend Dee will let Tim know where we are soon."

Each time we poked through the illusion, it was still a relief to find our hands attached when we pulled them back. "I'd say about six feet by three feet. I want to look before we go through it. Would you mind hanging on to me?"

I nodded. "I got ya!"

His upper half disappeared into the rock wall and then reappeared like he was doing a magic trick.

He grinned like a child. "It's the back of a waterfall. Come on."

As I stepped into the wall, the cool breeze of the rushing water dampened my skin, which looked the same shade of gray as the rocks because of the clever lighting. I squinted but couldn't make out what was ahead. Another step, though, was like Dorothy stepping out of her house after the tornado. It was beautiful behind the waterfall. We stood on a small ledge, and before us was a wall of water feeding into a blue pool. Sitting and watching the water cascade with a strawberry daiquiri would be incredible. Although it appeared safe and peaceful, I knew it wasn't.

"There's a rope here. I'm guessing they climb it. I'm going to swing down to the water. You follow me, okay?"

"Sure," I said.

Rob nodded and swung wide over the water and then let go. After a considerable splash, he surfaced with a big boyish grin.

"Join me." The rope swung back in my direction, and I grabbed it.

The thrill of swinging through the air and letting go was something I hadn't experienced since I was a young girl at the river. I flew and landed in the deep water. Soon we were out of the pond with the sun warming us. I squeezed the water out of my hair, blond streaks with red hiding those telltale gray strands. Well, I wasn't giving in to more than a few strands. I was fond of my high school hair color and paid good money for it.

"I felt like a kid again for a moment."

Rob scanned the area as I smiled. He shook his head. "Me too. We are living in a *Twilight Zone* episode for sure, but not the one you wanted. I can't process this now, except we need to get some answers. Let's keep moving and find our boat. See if it's damaged. But truthfully, I say we take our chances on the open seas rather than stay here longer in this craziness."

"It is crazy, but Tim was right. No one would believe us, so what does it matter?"

Rob squinted in the bright sun. "We know. That's all that matters."

Trudging through the big tropical confusion, we found the beach quickly.

"This way," Rob whispered and pointed to the left.

We followed it until we got back to our camp. There was the burned-out hull of our boat and a pile of our clothes, personal items, and kitchenware next to it.

"It was true," I gasped as Rob grabbed my hand and tugged us toward the safety of the trees.

A harsh voice called out from behind us. "What? No welcome for your guests?"

"Run, Gigi! Don't look back."

We nearly made it to the trees before a smiling, disheveled man in faded black shorts intercepted, holding a propane torch in one hand and a gun in the other. Both were pointed at us.

He winked with a horrible bloodshot eye. "We've been waiting for you. We wanted to thank you for the supplies. That nice ring looks to be worth some money." His smile transformed into a smirk that didn't reach his cold shark eyes.

"Ring?" I realized he meant my fortieth wedding anniversary ring, which cost a small fortune.

He nodded to someone behind us. "Yeah, that old thing on your left hand. You know, lady, the ring finger. Hand it over. And don't do anything stupid, mister. We'll let you two live if you don't cause us any trouble. We're going to leave this place soon."

I glanced at Rob. "We'll gladly give you the ring if you leave us alone," said Rob. "There's nothing of value left, from what I can see."

"I'll be the judge of that one, mister." He advanced cautiously toward us after putting the torch down. He held out his grimy free hand but kept his gun leveled at us. I tossed the ring into it, and his fingers closed over it like an oyster shell. My throat constricted, knowing it was gone forever.

I could smell the alcohol on his breath. "Luckily your wife is old and harmless. No one is attracted to her or you. But I can't trust a man not to be a man, so if I break one of your legs, you'll be harmless too."

Rob's eyes widened. "What? What can I do to you? You have a gun and all our stuff."

The man slipped the ring into his pocket and ran his hand through his long, brown hair. "Yup, that's probably true. But there's no guarantee you won't try some stupid Rambo thing, you know? You are old, but you look healthy to me. Old doesn't mean you ain't got no moves. Nothing personal. Then we're going to head out of here. Your lady will heal you up—or not. It's not my problem."

Another man, short, with jet-black hair and missing some teeth, came from behind a tree. He was holding a long pipe in his chubby hands. Rob looked at me with a deep grimace, sweat on his forehead. "Just don't hurt her."

"Hurt her? Why would we do that, Carl?"

"Wait! We promise—" I gasped as Carl held up the pipe and swung like he was going for a home run. A grubby hand grasped my arm painfully.

Carl connected to Rob's leg before I could even try to pull away. I couldn't help my husband. There was a crack, and a wounded-animal yell escaped from the man I'd loved most of my life. Before he even hit the ground, Carl got another swing in. Rob's eyes rolled back as he crumpled, groaning. His left leg was at an odd angle—it looked like a severe break. Rob remained silent as tears escaped from his eyes.

"Stay down, old man, or she gets it next," Carl said. He was smaller but looked meaner than the first guy with the cruel smile.

"We made a deal, Carl. *We* don't touch her. They ain't going to make it with her in charge, anyway."

"Sure, boss."

I ran to Rob's side, shaking my head as the words tumbled out, "Those reptile people were telling the truth! Oh, Rob!"

Rob shook his head at me through the pain. It was too late; I had mentioned the reptile people. Great, they might kill us because they thought we were insane.

The boss shook his head. "Those *what* people? You guys taking something extra in your vitamins?"

I didn't reply.

"You got dementia, lady. I wish I could watch this play out, mister, but we gotta go. Bye, folks! Good luck."

They ran off laughing into the jungle.

Rob wiped his eyes and grimaced. "It hurts like hell, Gigi. At least they didn't hurt you."

"I don't like your deal, and I wish I could have helped you. I've never felt so helpless in my life." The tears flowed, and I wiped them away.

Rob grunted as he adjusted his position. "I would have done anything to keep you safe. A broken leg seems worth it to me. I'm glad they thought you were crazy." A slight grin turned into a grimace of pain. "Can you find something to stabilize this leg so it can heal? I can make some crutches, and we'll be ready to go."

"Go where?" I asked gently.

"They may have burned the boat, but they left a few things over there, see? Our raft." Rob pointed and grunted.

The raft was melted into a lump, but I didn't mention that. "Lie still. I'll find some sticks and see what we have left to work with."

I kicked through the pile, but most things had been shredded. I only found a usable blanket, Rob's coat, a pair of my flip-flops, and a pillow. They had spent some time and energy on our things. At least they left us alive, but we still had to deal with the reptile people. We were screwed, basically.

Rob groaned as I helped him lie flat and put the pillow under his head. I tried to straighten his leg the best I could, but it hurt him every time I moved it. He never complained. Besides teaching history, I often helped with human anatomy classes, and that was helpful. Satisfied I had done all that was possible, I studied him as he closed his eyes. I worried he was going into shock—his breathing was rapid and his complexion was pale. It broke my heart to see him hurt.

"You'll have to stay here without moving until you heal," I mumbled as I placed his coat over him. "I got this."

Rob opened his eyes for a moment. "Do you think the aspirin survived?"

"I'll look for the aspirin. You rest."

Clouds approached from the horizon with the speed of a hurricane. Or was it the storm Tim mentioned? Not that it mattered now —what was done was done.

I picked through the rubble again and found the intact first aid kit buried deep under the shredded clothes and broken dishes. There was, thankfully, a new bottle of aspirin. Our luck was improving, until Tim found us. Then who knew? We weren't going anywhere, so we were at the mercy of those creatures. I handed Rob three pills. He chewed on them with a frown and then fell asleep.

I sighed and watched the approaching storm, knowing all our food and water were gone. I kicked the pile, hoping something new would appear, but nothing did. I searched through the charred wood and burned plastic of the boat. Nothing. Then a patch of blue by the tree line caught my eye. The sand didn't allow for a quick investigation. I was breathless by the time I discovered our tarp.

The dark clouds were suddenly on top of us. Rob was snoring lightly when they opened up. I wrapped the blue plastic material around us and waited it out. The rain falling on the tarp sounded like a machine gun.

"Just like a tent."

Lightning streaked across the sky, lighting everything up before the boom of the thunder that shook Rob awake. He moaned when he moved. "I hope that means they're gone now."

"I hope so, Rob. Good riddance to those sleazes."

Rob offered the weakest of smiles. "Stupid of me to come back here to prove a point, but it will be okay. My leg will heal fast, and I can get a boat built. My guess is those lizard things are done with us."

I offered a fake smile. His leg had already swollen. That wasn't a broken bone. It was a shattered bone, one that required surgery. It would never heal. "Yes, we're going to be fine."

A final clap of thunder roared, and then it was suddenly silent as the sun's warm rays took over the landscape. I pulled back the tarp like I was peeling a banana and was greeted with blue skies—and Tim holding a black stick and a plate.

"We were worried about you after Dee called in. We couldn't get here in time, sorry. Here, eat this, Rob. It will help you heal faster."

Rob peeked at the mound of green goop. "No, thanks. I'll be fine."

I looked into Tim's eyes. They showed a caring that had been absent in the men who did this to Rob. I had to put my trust some-where if we were going to survive. "Come on, honey, a couple of bites for me? Please?"

Rob tried to sit but threw up. He wiped his mouth with his hand as Tim crouched by his side, holding a spoon filled with green goop.

"Please, Rob. They wouldn't be helping if they wanted to hurt you, would they?"

Rob sighed and grabbed the offered spoon. Holding his breath, he shoveled it into his mouth. His eyes widened.

"It's good. Tastes like cherry."

Tim ran a small black box over Rob's body. "Our medicine is as good as our food." He slowed down over his leg and passed it several times. "Hmmm. He got not only your leg but your hip. Unfortunate swing. It will take a bit, but we'll heal you in a few days."

"This green goop will heal my bones?" Rob kept shoveling it into his mouth and smacking his lips.

"Yes, along with my scanner." Tim frowned, which made him look imposing.

"How could we know whom to trust?" Rob mumbled as he ran his fingers over the plate and licked them.

Tim shook his head and held his hands out. "The ones who help you with no strings attached. We had to knock them out and send them on their way. We didn't kill them. Although if we had, it wouldn't have been bad for your world, but not good for our new world. Those . . . men were watching you and laughing. They had no intention of leaving you alive after seeing them."

"Why?" I smoothed Rob's hair down.

Tim shrugged.

"You must understand why we left." Rob lay back down.

"Yes, I understand your fears. Luckily I knew where you would go. Sorry we couldn't help you sooner, but we had to finish removing them before we could get you the medicine and scanner."

"So you aren't angry with us?" I asked.

"No, just worried." Tim shook his head. "When Rob is healed, I will give you a full tour."

Overhead two large butterflies with alligator bodies but the same colorful wings as those on Earth circled above us and then flew away.

"Butterflies?" I exclaimed.

"Similar to yours, with a few minor exceptions."

"Beautiful." I looked down at Rob, whose face was contorted in pain when he tried to sit up.

Tim smiled. "They are."

Two dolphins jumped out of the water as a pair of brontosauruses peeked from the tree line.

"They are magnificent." I reached up to the butterflies, but they kept their distance.

"They are as curious about you as you are about them. I must take care of that break so it can heal right. Do you mind if I touch you, Rob?"

Rob shook his head and looked away. A loud buzz rumbled through my body, and the animals disappeared. I couldn't hold my eyes open. The next thing I knew, I was next to Rob, and his leg was wrapped in a big golden cloth secured with long metal ties. We were back in our room.

Tim peeked through the door with a smile.

"I'm glad you're awake. You should feel better, Rob. Here, let me help you sit up."

"Thank you. I do," Rob admitted.

"Healing works fast here, and we got your bones nicely lined up." Tim bent over and carefully wiped away a bit of dried green goo from around Rob's mouth. I wiped mine and found some too. How long had we both been out?

"Go slow. You should be fine soon."

Rob frowned. "Thank you for helping us."

"Yes, thank you," I added.

"You are both very welcome."

We spent the next couple of days sleeping and eating green goo that tasted like cheese pizza or fresh fruit. I always woke up refreshed, used the amazing restroom, and ended up dozing off again. I assumed they were caring for Rob's bathroom needs, but I could never stay awake long enough to ask.

Rob's leg healed quickly and looked healthy when it was unwrapped. Tim came in smiling.

"You should be fully healed, both of you."

"Um, both of us?" I asked, sitting up and stretching. There were none of the familiar pains.

"Yes, Rob's bones and muscles are repaired fully, along with his back. You had some issues in your spine, I believe. Our doctor checked you both out when you got here. And your cell issue, Gigi, has been reversed. So you're all ready."

"What cell issue? I got a clean bill of health at the doctor's last time."

"They missed something. It originated in your skin and moved into your bones. What was it called? Yes, cancer. If left alone, you would have only had a few months to live. Now you're fine." Tim smiled.

"She had what? Your doctor must be mistaken." Rob put his arm around me.

Tim's eyes widened. "Oh, no, he never makes mistakes. His equipment is foolproof. Maybe I shouldn't have mentioned this. Are you upset?"

I shook my head. "Upset? I'm not sure. I guess I'm happy it's gone if I had it. I thought the pain was from getting old."

"What pain?" Rob asked me.

"You know my back and feet have been giving me trouble after the break, and it moved into my hips and stomach. I thought—well, no matter now."

Tim smiled. "Great. Are you ready to return home soon? We've had enough time to make another storm and build you a boat. Unless you want to stay longer for that promised tour."

"I thank you for what you've done for us. Yes, we would like to get home, unless you want to do the tour, Gigi?"

"Home sounds good to me."

Rob stood slowly and tentatively moved around.

"Any pain? I could get our doctor." Tim asked.

"No. No pain at all." Rob smiled.

"Great. You have some clean clothes in the bathroom. I'm sure you'll want a shower too. I'll be back soon and get you to your boat."

We ran into the bathroom and locked the door behind us like two teenagers who finally had the house to themselves.

"I feel so—" Rob stopped my words with a deep kiss that continued in the shower. He was completely healed and reminded me of the man on my honeymoon as the water cascaded over our intertwined naked bodies in one of the longest showers we've ever taken.

"This is nuts," I said as we reluctantly got out.

Rob grinned. "Yeah, but good nuts. I've never felt better."

"Me either. Do you think I had cancer?" I pulled a soft, floral-scented blue towel around me.

"I can't think about that. That's why I had to be with you. Even thinking about losing you—" Rob's voice choked up.

We quickly dressed in silence and went back into the room to wait.

Tim peeked his head in. "Ready? Follow me."

We walked behind Tim from tunnel to tunnel to a dead end. We never saw the big room.

"This is it. Come on." Tim disappeared through the rock. We followed him into a small pond.

I swam through water at the perfect temperature until we reached the shore. I was more alive than I'd ever been. Pain-free. Such a fantastic feeling.

"We have exits without water, but this is closest to your new boat."

"How could you do that so fast?" I shook my head.

"We have some excellent tools. It's nearly identical to the one you had. I hope that works for you. We added some improvements, of course. This ship is borrowed, correct?"

Rob nodded.

Tim continued, "You tell that owner you were wrecked on an island but you're handy with a nail—or is it a hammer? Either way. We'll make a storm for you, and you'll be on your way. I'm honored to have met you. Follow the path through those trees. The boat is ready to go."

He held out his hand, and Rob took it. They both smiled at each other.

"Unless . . . " Tim said with a slight smile.

"Unless what?" I asked.

"We've gotten to know you both well. Our doctor assures us that you are both wonderful humans inside and out. We could use your help around here caring for the animals, if you're interested."

"You mean stay here?" I asked.

"Yes. I forgot to mention one side effect of your treatments. It slows your aging, giving you another forty-five healthy years. And, of course, some time has passed in your world."

"We'd be over 115 years old!" I frowned.

Rob pushed his mouth to one side. "What do people think happened to us back home? What do you mean some time has passed?"

"Well, you've been here a couple of weeks, but that's around 8.5 months on Earth time. From our information, you were declared missing and then presumed dead. We can pick up the local news most of the time. Your children held a funeral for you on the ocean. I thought it was rather nice when they released those two doves. You were declared dead in court right after. I assumed it was so the owner could get his boat replaced and your kids could take care of your things. Then we lost that channel of information, which we were getting through the Elders. Of course, your return would be a wonderful surprise, right? How happy your family would be to find you alive, and how grateful the owner would be to get his boat back."

"A surprise, indeed. I bet we have nothing to go home to. We'd be a charity case for our kids now. Not what I'd want, even though we'd be living on our money. Are you sure we'll live until we're 115 years old?"

"We went over the figures several times. That's on the low end. We've never had this problem before. No one has ever stayed around and had treatments. Besides, just being here is healing. Staying would add another two hundred years at least." Tim's face broke into a huge smile.

Rob frowned. "All our pets are gone. Our kids have their own lives. Our friends are moving into retirement communities. We'll miss our family, but our money has helped them now. We couldn't ask them to give it back, could we? Why didn't you tell us this at first?"

"We wanted to ensure you had a choice, to go or stay. We built your boat and offered you that. We thought your family would happily welcome you back."

"I'm sure they'd be happy, but . . . "

"He means they probably spent all our money. We'd be broke, and what a mess if we were declared dead! Wouldn't it be better if we stayed dead now?" I sighed.

Rob nodded. "So, um, what would we take care of if we stayed here?"

Tim looked at his wrist and punched in a response. "You mentioned your education, Gigi, and your love of dinosaurs, Rob. Gigi could teach our children about Earth, and Rob could help care for the dinosaurs. We'd start you with the grass eaters, then slowly move to some of the more dangerous ones. It will be a long time before we can return to our own planet, if ever."

I caught Tim's gaze. "I feel like you wanted us to stay from the beginning."

He shrugged. "I must admit, I've grown quite fond of you and would welcome your company, if that helps."

Rob pursed his lips. "Can we talk?"

"Please do. I will be over in that grove checking on the elephants. Holler when you're ready." He walked away without looking back.

I ran my fingers through my hair. It had grown three inches since we'd been here. "What should we do? How could we explain living so long? It would be fun, but how could we afford it without returning to work? Now that we've been declared dead, you know the money's gone. Our family has already grieved our death. Honestly, I'm scared." My voice shook as my fear burned in my throat.

Rob gently caressed my cheek. "I know you'll be surprised as we switch responses here, but this is our second chance. On some level, I know Tim is telling the truth. Don't you feel that?"

"Yes," I admitted as all my fear flowed away. I wasn't the same as when I arrived, and that moment reminded me of that. "It's still scary, though."

"It is, and I haven't lost my skeptical side. But Tim said something he could only have known from watching our news. Something I asked Sasha to do for me when I died. I've never even told you. It seemed silly."

"What's that?" I asked, tilting my head back.

"I asked her to release a dove at my funeral. And at yours. Tim said two were released from a boat. She did what I asked."

"Oh." I felt my throat tighten. I would miss them.

"They've grieved for us and moved on. Disrupting their lives and living so long isn't fair. No. Too weird."

I smiled. "Maybe there's a way to peek in on them, as Tim did."

Rob smiled. "Won't hurt to ask. So, what do you think? Continue our adventure like we started, just the two of us?"

"Yes, but how will we pay for things here?" I asked.

Rob shrugged. "Sounds like we'll have jobs, but let's find out. Tim!"

Tim laughed when Rob asked about money. "No money required

here. We all do our part, and that works out. You can always leave later if you choose, but the longer you stay, the harder it will be to explain your robust health. One more thing to consider—every moment you live here will be healthy. Sickness isn't an issue until it's time for your body to stop working."

"Could we leave, check on our family later, and then come back?" I asked.

"You could. But there's no guarantee you'll find us again. We don't have a traveling rock like those bird people—there was no reason to have one. I suppose we could ask the Elders, but they will likely not agree to that. Every world is different."

Rob stayed behind me and wrapped his arms around my waist. I leaned against him. "Could we peek in on them as you did?"

"Yes, I think we can arrange that."

"Then we'll stay," I declared.

"I am so happy to hear that. Now come meet the rest of us, and we'll set you up with a place to live that has a door. I look forward to your Earth lessons, Gigi."

"I'd love to be in the classroom again."

"Great—you have a lot to teach us. Later I'll give you both that animal tour. There are some dinosaurs eager to meet you."

Our new adventure continued, filled with the spark that life used to provide. Someday I'd be reunited with my loved ones in another place, I reassured myself, but right now we were having the time of our lives.

Author's Note

I HOPE you enjoyed the story collection. The ideas bloomed from challenges or stories that didn't work as a novel. The ninety-nine-word stories were written for a challenge from Carrot Ranch Literary Community. Although not all of them made the challenges, I enjoyed making a story in limited words. Some stories were written for the amazing and missed Suzanne Burke's 'Fiction In A Flash Challenge.' They were under 750 words, but I might have added a few more words to them while working on this book. The dedications are to family members. I had them give me a word, and I'd search for an image under that word. The stories flowed from that chosen image. *Stranded* is my grownup version of *An Unusual Island*. What if adults on the other end of the aging process got stranded in a place where nothing was what it seemed? It's a happily ever after for those who think there's nothing left.

About the Author

D. L. Finn is an independent California local who encourages everyone to embrace their inner child. She was born and raised in the foggy Bay Area, but in 1990 she relocated with her husband, kids, dogs, and cats to Nevada City, in the Sierra foothills. She immersed herself in reading all types of books but especially loved romance, horror, and fantasy. She always treasured creating her own reality on paper. Finally, surrounded by towering pines, oaks, and cedars, her creativity was nurtured until it bloomed. Her creations include children's books, adult fiction, a unique autobiography, and poetry. She continues on her adventure with an open invitation to all readers to join her.

EXCERPT FROM This Second Chance

Angels & Evildwels Series Book 1

THEY HOVERED over the familiar woman in the wedding dress. She looked terrified, and on the day that she should be at her happiest.

"You are getting a chance most do not get. You understand that, right?" Zelina asked.

He meekly nodded at her. Her brown eyes narrowed, piercing his soul. She clearly didn't like him—not that he blamed her.

"Good. We are clear. You give Rachael her happy ending. Then you can move on and let go of *some of* that bad you did," Zelina said, pursing her lips tightly together.

Her pale silver gown flowed around her like an ocean wave ebbing in and out. He never understood how angels' clothes did that yet, at the same time, kept their form enough to cover them modestly.

"I understand, and I'm grateful I've been given this second chance. I won't let you, or Rachael, down. I'll do whatever it takes to make it happen," he replied, more confidently than he felt.

Although it confused him that he was being given this chance, he'd never question this angel. He certainly didn't deserve it and hadn't had a moment's peace since his death. Everything he'd done flashed before him—over and over. He was relieved to have a break from it and a chance to finally do some good, but he was merely a ghost—a soul, or a man without a body. What could he do to take away that expression on Rachael's face?

"Yes, it is a break from your much-earned reflections." Zelina crossed her arms, obviously irritated at him.

He felt his face redden as he nodded back at her. In this form he felt all the physical and emotional reactions he had when he was alive, but stronger. He needed to remember that angels always knew what he was thinking. He had no privacy now.

"I had to watch Rachael make some bad mistakes. I will not do this again; this is too important. You must figure out how to fix this and make your atonement. You know the rules. If I see you doing any harm, I will send you back. This is your *only* chance to do some good. I will be watching if you need some guidance, but I think you will figure it out," Zelina finished, suddenly seeming taller to him.

Her black hair glowed as she put her hands on her hips with her wings fully extended. He never tired of seeing the shimmering, feathered wings that reminded him of a peacock tail. They were beautiful. Under all that splendor, he knew, there was a ferociousness akin to a bear protecting her young. Rachael was her cub.

When her wings were tucked behind her, unseen, Zelina seemed perfectly ordinary. She could walk among the humans unnoticed. She turned her gaze on him again and scowled. She oversaw people like him—the tough cases. He sighed. Zelina responded to his sigh with a smirk. On Earth that look would have infuriated him, coming from a woman. Now it scared him.

A sudden chill ran through him. "Is someone else here?" he asked.

"It is not a someone; it is more of a thing, and it is what you are up against. It has no conscience, unlike even someone like you; your conscience peeked out after your reign of terror. This thing has no empathy, no love—only hate. I cannot hear what it thinks. It is the purest form of evil and is called an *evildwel*. This one has consumed its human—even in death. You had one in control of you, but a part of you remained. Death might have saved you, or you might have fought it off someday. I do not know things like that. What I do know is that this evildwel means Rachael harm. Be careful, and do not disappoint me," Zelina warned, and then she vanished.

In the corner of the room, there was no form for him to make out, only thick, dark mist. Did the evildwel know he was there? He suddenly wished Zelina hadn't left him. He was afraid, yet he was going to do what Zelina requested—not because he had no choice, but because he had a lot of things to make up for. It was time to get to work.

Rachael's detachment from the image in the mirror smoothing the satin, off-white wedding gown puzzled her. After all, this was the same scalloped three-quarter dress, showing off her newly trim waist, that she'd pictured herself in after seeing it on a *Bridal* magazine cover over twenty years ago. Frowning, Rachael adjusted the tiny yellow roses and baby's breath in her Gibson-styled, lightened auburn hair with her set of pink, acrylic nails.

"Not bad for age thirty-seven and three kids," Rachael tried to reassure the pale image in the mirror.

It didn't work. The urge to rip off the dress and fake nails and make a dash out the back door was even stronger now.

"Why?" Rachael asked the woman staring back at her in the mirror, unaware of her unseen visitors.

Rachael couldn't have asked for a more perfect day. The weather, the gazebo Tony had built for their ceremony, the dress that her mother had spent hours making for her—everything in her life had finally fallen into place. It was perfect. Maybe this was just a very delayed reaction to her first wedding. That was when the strong urge to run out the back door would have come in handy. But if she'd done that, her kids wouldn't be here. Besides, Rachael couldn't compare this June morning to that snowy December day nineteen years ago when she'd stood holding a stale bouquet of faded satin flowers at some nameless chapel in Reno.

Rachael sighed and felt a chill shoot through her, even though the room was over 75 degrees. Stress, she concluded. Careful not to wrinkle her satin dress, she sat in the old maple rocking chair and pulled the handmade pink comforter over her. The comforter had been made by Tony's mother, Nora. She raised Tony alone after his father, Wayne Battaglia, died in a horrible car crash when Tony was barely a year old. Tony knew very little about his father, and his mother had never talked about him to her son. Tony was convinced this was due to grief and never pressed for information. Rachael thought his mother's response, not to tell a son about his father, was strange. One thing Rachael was positive about was that Nora had done a fantastic job raising Tony into the man he was.

Unlike her first mother-in-law, who'd raised (well, at least given birth to) Ed. Tammy kept food on the table and a roof over his head by helping make meth in a lab next door to their trailer. When she finally walked away from that addiction, she turned to others: drinking and pain pills. Tammy always had a man in her life. Some of them helped raise Ed; others didn't. Ed hadn't been sure if one of them was his father. He wasn't sure if his mother knew, either.

After Rachael gave birth to their first son, Eddie, Tammy had confided to her in an emotionless tone, "Al, this man I was seeing, fooled around with little Ed, if you know what I mean. I think he was eight or something like that. I didn't stand for that crap. I kicked Al right out on his ass, I did. I'm glad Ed grew up to like women. Never know which way they'll go after that. You keep an eye on little Eddie Jr., here, so you can have grandkids someday too," Tammy added with a nod, as though she had imparted some heavy wisdom to Rachael. Tammy then brushed her frizzy, bottle-blond hair out of her face and took a long drink from her vodka-scented orange juice.

Rachael had been horrified and tried to talk to Ed about it. He'd refused and made sure his mother knew to never bring that subject up again. Rachael understood he had good reason to be angry. What she didn't understand was why it was directed at her and not at the people who'd hurt him. The one good thing Tammy had done for Rachael and her kids was to stay out of their lives after the divorce. Tammy had even left the planning of her only child's funeral in Rachael's hands. Rachael had been shocked when her ex-mother-in-law didn't even attend Ed's funeral because it fell during happy hour.

The motherly rhythm of the rocking chair wasn't easing Rachael's anxiety. The turmoil she had thought she was rid of when she signed the divorce papers still haunted her. After Ed's funeral a couple of years ago, she thought she had *finally* found closure—guess not. Images from those dark days slammed at her like Ed's fist used to do when he drank too much.

The most predominant image was falling snow. Snow was something Rachael had only seen on TV (until her first wedding) because it didn't snow in the Bay Area, where she grew up. There was one exception, of course (because there always is an exception with everything, Rachael learned quickly), when she was in junior high school. It had snowed for five minutes and melted in even less time.

So when her first soon-to-be husband, Ed, suggested, with his best smile, "What do you say to going to Reno, building us a snowman, and tying the knot?" Rachael had quickly agreed. To be a bride *and* see the snow seemed perfect. Neither Rachael nor Ed had much money; they were both freshly out of high school. So Rachael bought her wedding dress off the discount rack at the local department store. She found a light-silver prom dress at 75 percent off that covered her already bulging belly. They got into his old, beat-up, red Chevy pickup and drove. The snow at the summit was beautiful and magical. When they got to the "biggest little city in the world," it started to snow. She had been convinced this meant they would have a long and happy life.

Ed had a fake ID so he could gamble, and he won big. They went out for a steak dinner at a fancy restaurant at the casino to celebrate and got a room that overlooked Reno. She'd watched the snow fall from the eleventh floor with Ed by her side. She was completely at peace. The next morning, they went to the chapel in the hotel and got married.

Things went downhill the moment they returned home. A few years later, Rachael (who had just found out she was pregnant again) grabbed her two small children and escaped when her husband wasn't home. They only had the clothes they were wearing when they found safety at a local women's shelter.

"What am I doing?" Rachael exclaimed, jumping out of the rocking chair. "This is going to be the happiest day of your life, Rachael, whether you like it or not! This just has to be those prewedding jitters they always talk about." The wide-eyed figure in the mirror didn't look convinced. "Besides, all the important people in your life are waiting for you downstairs! Well, not everyone..." Rachael sank heavily back down into the chair.

Eddie wasn't going to be there, all because of a comment Rachael had made to his girlfriend a couple of months ago.

"If you need *anything*, you can always come to me, understand? My door is always open to you. You have a place to go." Rachael hugged Sasha goodbye before going down to bail Eddie out of jail.

He'd gotten into a brawl at a bar where he shouldn't have legally been. She promised herself this would be the last time she'd help him until he helped himself.

Unfortunately, when Eddie finally got released (and later put on probation), Sasha repeated what Rachael had said. Eddie didn't see it as a sweet gesture, like Sasha did. He caught the intended warning. He cut his family out of his and Sasha's lives—just like his dad had done.

Ed had moved Rachael away from her family right after they eloped. Los Angeles was a seven-hour drive from her family and friends. It was a place Rachael had never got used to living in. But Rachael could be wrong about Sasha and Eddie. He certainly didn't move her away from her friends, and she had no family to cut out of their lives after her parents died, although Rachael could see Eddie becoming more like his dad every day, with drugs, drinking, and stealing, which worried her.

Just over two months ago, Rachael still believed Eddie would change his mind and come to the wedding. He hadn't. Rachael's calls were screened by an answering machine, and her messages were never answered. In one final attempt last week, Rachael tried dropping off a birthday gift to Eddie at his apartment. To Rachael's surprise, Sasha opened the door.

"I'm sorry, Rachael. I must honor Eddie's wishes and not let you in or take the present. It's his birthday, and I don't want to upset him. You understand, don't you?" Sasha asked with a weak smile.

Sasha looked like she was coming down with the flu. She was as pale as her white-blond hair. Rachael held back her questions on Sasha's health. It wouldn't help the tensions between her and Eddie if he thought Rachael was suggesting more than the flu.

"Yes, Sasha. I understand perfectly. But if you would just tell Eddie—well, maybe don't tell him I came by. I'll try coming back when he's home. Thank you, Sasha."

"You're right. I don't want to spoil his nineteenth birthd—I didn't mean it to come out like that! It's just that Eddie is cleaning himself up. He wanted one more celebration tonight. Eddie's gonna quit drinking. He brought home some catalogs from colleges to go through. Tomorrow we're deciding where he's going to school. Oh, I forgot about Eddie's cake in the oven. I hope you have a wonderful wedding day. Sorry we can't make it. We'll be in touch soon, but maybe you shouldn't drop by anymore unless you talk to him first—sorry," Sasha said, quickly shutting the door.

Hurt, Rachael climbed back into her blue SUV. She prayed Sasha was right about Eddie cleaning up. Rachael had tried to help him, as had her mother, the counselors, and Sasha—but only Eddie could overcome this. What if that therapist at the women's shelter was right? She said that Eddie, at six years old, couldn't be helped—he was too far gone. Rachael thought the woman was not only rude but completely wrong. Eddie had been in therapy for that first year, after she left Ed. It was fine for a while, until Rachael began to see signs that he might be taking after his dad. By that time Eddie was refusing all help. Ed was coming around and playing the victim card with his oldest son.

Rachael finally had to change the child visitation rights. Ed was only allowed to see the kids on supervised visits, twice a month. She always felt Ed found a way around this with Eddie, but she could never prove it. Eddie was as good at lying as his father. More therapy followed Ed's death, with no results, even with the medications. Eddie always slipped back into his bad behavior, until he was kicked out of school in his senior year—then he moved out.

It was painful to have her oldest son push her out of his life. Rachael sighed as a single tear flowed down her cheek. She quickly wiped it away, right as her mother burst into the room.

"I finished Kelly's hair," Mae announced. "She looks like an angel, and so does her mom."

"Thanks-s, Mom," Rachael said, hopping up from the chair and rushing to check her hair again. *No more bad thoughts. Today marks the wedding I have always dreamt of,* Rachael thought, staring at the bride in the mirror, who returned her look with a phony smile. "Where's Kelly?"

"She's in the bathroom. Probably fixing her hair exactly like you used to do after I styled it. Like all girls do, I guess." Mae grinned.

"Well, I could use some help. Do you think we should put more flowers in my hair, or less? Should I put the back down, or leave it all up?" Rachael was relieved to be back in action.

"I think you look perfect. I wouldn't touch a thing, except for this," Mae said as she held out a box.

"What is it?" Rachael asked.

"Open it," Mae encouraged with a smile.

Rachael ripped through the pink paper. It was a ring box. In it was the 1.5-carat, square-cut diamond set in white gold that her father had given to her mother on their thirtieth wedding anniversary. When he died five years ago, her mother had put it away and started wearing her old gold wedding band on a chain around her neck.

"Oh, Mom! I can't take this!"

"You can, and you will. Tony and I had this conversation a long time ago when he asked me for your hand in marriage. Besides, the Lord only blessed me with one daughter and one son. I plan to spoil them both as much as their father spoiled me. So you have your wedding ring, you are wearing the blue garter, which is also new, and your pearl necklace is borrowed and old. You're set. Now all I have to do is deliver you to that gem waiting for you in your gazebo."

Rachael smiled. Her mother had loved Tony the minute she met him. The fact that he was Italian, like Rachael's father, was a big selling point for Mae. For the last four years, she had fussed over Tony like he was her long-lost child. It was such a relief to Rachael that she had fallen helplessly in love with Tony—her mother would have been lost without him.

"Is Stevie dressed?" Rachael asked.

"Yes. I already got some wonderful pictures of him and Tony—I mean, Dad, now. They look so handsome. Oh, I forgot. There's a small box that came for you this morning. A note on it said, 'Open Now.' Bet it's something from your husband-to-be. I'd better get it."

Rachael's mother seemed to float out of the room. Rachael grinned when she noticed a similarity between cotton candy at the fair and her mother in her long, pink gown. That shade of pink was Mae's favorite color. Rachael's dad always said that when her mother wore pink, he always had good luck. Rachael hoped this worked for her, too.

Kelly pushed past her exiting grandmother and straight into Rachael's arms. "Mom! You look so beautiful!"

Thank heavens Kelly had her dad's dark looks, but not his dark moods. She was the most even-tempered of her kids, and also the most stubborn. She tugged impatiently at her pink, rose-covered dress cuffs, which were too short. Rachael's mother swore that Kelly had grown an inch just last week, and she couldn't let them out any more before the wedding. Rachael and Kelly knew the dress was too small. Mae thought of Kelly as perpetually ten years old, but she was fourteen.

"Thank you, Kelly. You look good, yourself. I don't know if I should let you out there; you might take away all my attention," Rachael teased.

"No one will be looking at me today." Kelly shook her head.

"I hope you're right." Rachael beamed at her daughter.

"I am. Where'd Grandma go?" Kelly asked, checking her hair one more time.

Rachael glanced at the doorway. "Grandma went to get a package that came for me this morning."

"Here it is," Mae said, coming back with a small box and handing it to Rachael.

"This isn't Tony's handwriting," Rachael commented. No return address, but it had been sent to Tony's house. No—it wasn't going to be Tony's house anymore; it was going to be *her* house now, too. That was what Tony kept telling her over and over. It didn't seem real yet.

"Well, another wedding gift to add to the rest. Kelly, you'd better go downstairs with your brother for a few pictures. It's almost time for you to lead your mom down the aisle," Mae said as her soft doe eyes teared up.

"Why don't you open the present first?" Kelly insisted.

"No time. Besides, you need to get downstairs and get things ready. You have a bigger job to do as flower girl since the sick twins had to stay home. Those dresses were so cute on them, too! Can you believe that *both* sets of twins have the chicken pox?" Mae paused for a moment, so Rachael shook her head. Satisfied, she continued. "They should have gotten the shots for it. Oh well, at least Kathy, Patrick, and the boys made it, right? Now scoot, Kelly, and don't forget your flower basket," Mae finished breathlessly, making shooing motions with her hands.

"Okay," Kelly replied with a glance at her mom. She rolled her eyes. Yes, she was too old to be a flower girl, but she was playing along for her grandmother. At least she was head flower girl, they'd joked. "See you downstairs!" Kelly dashed out the door.

"Stay clean," Mae warned, but Kelly was, thankfully, long gone. "What else do you need, Rachael?"

"Nothing. I think I'm ready," Rachael said, but her eyes kept returning to the package. "I can't wait. I have to open this and see who it's from." She tore through the brown mailing paper and found a beautifully wrapped box underneath. "Isn't this paper pretty? Look! There are tiny gazebos on the paper. It must be from Tony! Maybe someone else addressed it for him."

"That would be like him. What is it?" Mae asked, trying to peek in the box.

"This isn't from Tony," Rachael quietly informed her mother. Her icy hands shook as she took the gift out of the box and handed it to her mother.

"A snow globe? Who'd send you this? Why, it's—" Mae said.

"Yes, it's the same snow globe Ed gave to me on our wedding day. It was the snowman he promised me. I thought we got rid of this years ago." Rachael shook her head in disbelief as her heart started racing.

"We did. I helped you take it to the charity myself. It must be another one just like it, a coincidence. Who sent it?" Mae asked, putting her hand on Rachael's arm.

Rachael quietly shrugged and took back the snow globe, studying it.

"Mom, something is written on the bottom of the globe. 'Remember'," Rachael whispered and dropped the globe onto the hardwood floor. It cracked open on impact and rolled into a small wooden table next to the bed, decapitating the snowman, and the severed head rolled under the bed. Shimmering goo splattered all over the satin mauve comforter.

"Don't walk in it, honey. You could slip. Thank my pink luck this didn't get all over you! I'll clean this up." Mae sprang into action. "Here, you'd better touch up your lipstick. Your brother, Kathy, and the boys just pulled up—late, as usual. It's eight forty-five already. The wedding starts at 9:00 a.m. sharp. We'd better get down there. Hurry."

Rachael numbly did as she was told and spread pink lipstick over her lips. But her feet wouldn't take her out of the feminine room with its lace doilies cradling the mauve lamps. This gift was a bad omen; her mother's "pink luck" wasn't working. Limp, Rachael sank back into the rocking chair. She watched as her mother dabbed up the last of the fake snowflakes on the floor and bundled up the comforter. Her mood had darkened and filled her body with a foreboding that she hadn't felt in years.

"I'll run this comforter through the wash later to make sure it doesn't stain. Now, you put this strange prank out of your mind. Don't let anything ruin *your* day. Please!"

"But Mom, it's as if Ed..." Rachael couldn't say the words she'd been thinking, that Ed was reaching out from the grave.

"Ed's gone. I saw him myself, in that coffin, where he belonged. But you know, little Eddie might have something to do with this."

"No, Mom. How could he know about this globe? I put it in the top part of my closet after he was born for safekeeping. I didn't see it again until I got out of the shelter and picked up those boxes that Ed left in the apartment. Then we got rid of everything that Ed hadn't ruined, and the snow globe was in one of them. We only took the kids' clothes when we flew home with you," Rachael said, feeling like her whole world was crashing down on her.

"Yes, we did get rid of all that stuff. Oh, Rachael, if you hadn't been so far away from me, I could have—you—but..." Rachael's mother faltered for an uneasy moment. "But now isn't the time for all of this! Shame on both of us! There must be a good reason for this. Right now, I don't care what the reason is, or who sent it! No one is going to ruin your day! And none of this 'reaching out from the grave' nonsense. Now, give me a hug, and let's go get you married!"

Rachael smiled and held onto her mother, taking in her floral scent. It was soothing. Mae was right; this wasn't the time. And after today, it would *never* be the time for it again. Rachael and her matron of honor, her mother, hurried downstairs. It was a family wedding, including Ava (who was like her sister), whose job was to play the song Tony had written for their wedding on his new Martin acoustic guitar while Rachael walked down the aisle. Ava began playing the song the moment Rachael stepped on the last stair and entered the kitchen to make her grand entrance out the back door.

Rachael's second wedding began with the oldest flower girl on record (that term had become a personal joke between her and Kelly) leading the procession. Rachael walked slowly down the aisle, covered in red rose petals, with her mother at her side. Not proper—the matron of honor should have led Rachael down the aisle—but Rachael wanted to do this *her* way today. Her brother, Patrick, could've taken their father's place at her side, but he was Tony's best man, and his sons, twelve-year-old Paddy and nine-year-old Sammy, were serving as ushers. At least Rachael hoped they were; she hadn't looked up yet. Couldn't. She felt that if she did, everything would be taken away from her.

"Isn't Kelly sweet?" Mae whispered to her as a couple of *oohs* and *ahhs* came from the guests.

"Like her grandma," Rachael whispered and forced her eyes to look up.

Kelly didn't disappear as Rachael watched her stroll ahead of them. Each step was perfect as she left a trail of rose petals. Rachael's eyes watered. Now that she had overcome her fear, tears were going to be the new problem. Rachael was *not* going to cry and ruin her makeup, not with all the cameras trained on her!

Mae squeezed her arm, sending a shock down her body. That was just what her father used to do when he was trying to cheer up Rachael or Patrick. She could clearly picture her father beaming down from heaven in approval at his family. He would have an extra twinkle in his eyes for his beloved wife in her pink dress. Rachael was smiling as they came to a stop at the gazebo.

She sent a silent message. *I love you, Daddy.*

It was time for Mae to hand her over to Tony. She tenderly kissed Rachael's cheek and put her cold hand into Tony's outstretched, warm one. Rachael immediately locked eyes with Tony. Everything disappeared but him.

She felt no qualms about doing this; love flowed through the rose-covered gazebo, the twenty guests, family members, and the priest. Her anxiety forgotten, Rachael had never felt safer in her life, except for when she was little and her mother or father could take her into their arms and make all the bad go away. Before Rachael knew it, she was saying "I do" and kneeling before the priest for the final blessing.

After they shared a shy kiss in front of the guests, Father Michael made the introduction: "May I present Mr. and Mrs. Battaglia."

This was met with clapping and whistles. Tony kissed her again, not as shyly as before. Suddenly, they were crushed by hugs, with Rachael's mother leading the way. Ava got the last hug in.

"I'm so happy for you, Rachael. You deserve all the happiness in the world," she said, sniffling.

"It almost seems too good to be true—" Rachael started to say.

"It isn't. You've earned this one many times over. And don't forget me, now that you've inherited an opal mine named Tony," Ava said with a laugh.

"I did," Rachael agreed with a grin. Opals were Ava's favorite stone; their fiery colors reminded Rachael of her best friend's personality. She added, somberly, "I'd never forget you. Only you and my parents were there for me when I reached out."

Ava shrugged and then added, with a wink, "Well, it looks like you'll be reaching out tonight and doing some mining." She pulled Rachael into another quick hug and then broke away and grabbed Kelly, who grinned at her mom, into her embrace.

"I believe you owe me a dance, Mrs. Battaglia." Tony claimed his bride.

"I believe I do, Mr. Battaglia," Rachael said. Boy, it sure felt good to be called "Mrs. Battaglia."

Tony nodded to Ava, who rushed back to the guitar. She

quickly began playing the song Tony and Rachael had shared their first kiss to, *Before You*. Ava's honeyed voice carried over the microphone and silenced the party. Tony held Rachael tightly, making her feel like nothing bad could ever happen if she was with him. They slowly glided over the backyard's freshly cut grass to the rhythm of the guitar. Rachael couldn't wait to get her high heels off, but for her wedding, she could stand it another hour or so. She was almost as tall as Tony at five feet ten inches in her heels (or "hells," as she liked to call them). Ava had run across these shoes, which went with her dress, last week, and they looked perfect—painful or not.

Tony nuzzled her cheek with his strong, Italian nose, and their eyes met. He was the most beautiful man Rachael had ever seen. His sloping, golden-brown eyes rarely flickered with anger; instead, they were creased at the corners as a sign of someone who always had a smile on his face. His wavy hair was under control today, thanks to some hair gel and Ava, even with the slight ocean breeze. Usually, his hair was endearingly tousled. The only imperfection Rachael could find was a small scar above his right eye, a reminder of a trip over the handlebars on his mountain bike on their third date.

"I love you, Rachael Battaglia," Tony whispered.

"I love you too," Rachael choked out.

Suddenly Tony dropped Rachael into a deep dip. The clicking sounds of cameras filled the air. Rachael caught her breath as she came back up and laughed, only to be dipped again. This time, Rachael had time to look around and noted how nice the house looked with its newly painted white trim from their sprucing-up party a few weeks ago. She was about to pull her glance away when she saw a shadow in the window of the bedroom where she'd just gotten dressed. No, it wasn't a shadow. It looked like a bearded man, but his facial features were darkened or perhaps blocked, like he was taking a picture. Unsure of what she was seeing, a sudden chill shot through her just as her husband pulled her upright.

"I think someone is taking pictures from your bedroom," Rachael commented, glancing around the backyard. All the guests seemed to be accounted for.

"That's because we're such a good-looking couple. They want to get all our angles, and it's *our* bedroom now," Tony added and twirled her around while the photographer snapped picture after picture until their song ended.

The morning was going by fast under a perfect June sun that pleasantly lit up the worn, dark wood of the two-story house that was to be her new home. Tony's mother, Nora, had been fond of mauve and dark brown, while Rachael had always leaned toward yellow and white. Tony had already suggested a redecorating party when they got back from their honeymoon. He didn't care if the whole house was bright pink, like everything in her mom's house, as long as Rachael was in it. She was so lucky.

When Ava finished her set of songs for dancing, the caterers served brunch. It was a huge spread of eggs, bacon, sausages, pancakes, waffles, French toast, potatoes, egg casseroles, and fruit—all of Rachael's and Tony's favorite foods. Soon it would be time to leave, after a delicate exchange of cake (cramming cake into someone's face wasn't the best of ways to start a life together, Rachael and Tony believed).

The wedding was ending, and the honeymoon waited to begin, even if it meant getting on a plane. Rachael's doctor had given her a prescription to help her through the flight. Her last flight had been to come home with her mother and kids after leaving Ed. She would have drunk her way through the trip if she hadn't been pregnant. Even though it was only an hour and a half, she was almost crawling out of her skin by the time they landed in Oakland. This trip out of San Francisco would be different, Rachael hoped.

Patrick made the toast. "May my baby sister and new brother, Tony, live happily ever after."

Kathy, her sister-in-law, piped in. "At least until you get home from the honeymoon and pick up your kids!"

Kelly loved going to her aunt and uncle's house. She and Kathy both had a love for all things paranormal, especially shows about ghosts and hauntings. Rachael knew they'd have a ghost movie marathon this week. Stevie, on the other hand, had bonded with his uncle. They both loved building things, just like Rachael's father. Kathy had assured her that she wouldn't notice either one of them mixed in with their six kids, who ranged in age from three to twelve years old, especially "whatshisname"—Stevie. Kathy loved to tease Stevie, who was the spitting image of Rachael's dad. He always played along.

They were amazingly tireless parents. Rachael didn't know how they did it, and they made it seem easy, too. She hoped it was something that would rub off on her and Tony. At least Rachael wouldn't have to worry about being away from her kids for the first time since she'd had Kelly.

The next toast came from Tony's only living relative in America, his mother's sister, Lee, who lived in San Francisco. Tony had only been around his aunt during the holidays when he was growing up. She was distant but made a point of making it to their wedding. Her blessing was in Italian, so Rachael didn't understand a word of it.

Aunt Lee had two boys around his age. Tony warned Rachael they wouldn't come to the wedding, and they hadn't. Tony hadn't been invited to their weddings years ago—nor had his mother. His aunt's explanation was that they'd had small weddings.

Tony confided once to Rachael that his cousins acted like he and his mother had a contagious disease.

"Jack and Steve were always polite, but they seemed like they wanted to leave the moment they walked in the door," he told Rachael and shrugged. "I haven't seen them since they graduated from high school. But we do exchange Christmas cards."

Well, with a strange mom like Lee, how could anyone expect the kids to be normal? Rachael thought, studying the woman. *Who wears black to a wedding, anyway?* In addition to her style choices, Aunt Lee sat apart and kept glancing at her watch. She would be the first to leave, Rachael determined. What really held the woman's attention, though, were the upstairs windows. Did she see someone up there too? Maybe it was time to introduce herself and ask. Rachael started making her way to her table.

She smiled and nodded as she passed by guests. She wondered if Tony's father's family had been as odd. They were killed in a helicopter crash right after he graduated high school. They were both teachers, like his father. It ran in the family, even though that was all she knew about that side.

Rachael had almost made her way to Aunt Lee when the woman suddenly stood up and rushed into the house. Was she avoiding Rachael, or did she suddenly have to use the restroom? Rachael sighed. It felt like Aunt Lee was avoiding her, and she understood Tony's comment about being treated like they had a contagious disease. Fine.

Rachael spotted her only other family members. Her mother's rich brother and his wife had moved to Arizona from San Diego (where Rachael's family used to spend vacations at the beach, visiting them). Her uncle and aunt were too busy eating, as usual, to join in the toasts. The remaining people were from work, except for Ava and her husband number two, Tim. He turned out to be the husband who had Ava talking about wanting children. Right now, though, Ava sat, surprisingly quiet, next to Mae. Rachael had thought Ava would say something at the toast, at least a quick joke, but instead, she had smiled with tears in her eyes and raised her glass to her. Rachael reciprocated.

Rachael made her final rounds through the rented banquet tables covered with pink flowers that, of course, her mother had helped pick out. Rachael smiled when she saw that Tony was in deep conversation with Patrick. From the way Patrick was demonstrating air fishing, she knew they were discussing their upcoming trip at the end of the summer. Rachael would then be in this house without Tony, the house his mother had bought after inheriting some money from her late aunt, who had left nothing to Aunt Lee. Maybe that was the issue? Nora had moved her seventeen-year-old son from San Francisco to Rachael's hometown, Pacifica. Tony said once that his only regret was leaving all his friends behind, but his mother was happy from the day she moved in, so it was worth it to him—once he got over the move. It was too bad they hadn't met earlier in life. He went off to school, and she got married, but finally they'd found each other.

Tony said he had never been married because he'd never found his soulmate until he met Rachael. At least, that was the story he told her, and Rachael chose to believe it. Luckily for Rachael, Tony had been a very devoted only child to his mother, and now that devotion passed to her.

Rachael knew she was the luckiest girl on Earth, even if she did have to walk through fire to get to this point. Speaking of fire, Rachael finally released her feet from her hells and watched Aunt Lee leave the party. She already didn't like one of her new relatives. She quickly headed back to her table and sat down next to her husband, who had another glass of champagne waiting for her. She didn't drink it; she'd already had two glasses during the toasts.

Ava came up behind Rachael, startling her.

"Time to throw that bouquet, Mrs. Battaglia," Ava said.

She heard Tim telling Tony the very same thing about the garter. As soon as Kelly caught the yellow roses and Bob, a teacher colleague of Tony's, caught the garter, their morning wedding came to an end.

Rachael and Tony ran to his truck through a steady rain of birdseed. Tony's truck had been decorated with a "Just Married" sign in the back window and pencils and erasers tied to the back. Rachael was sure she had Ava and Kelly to thank for that.

She had spent the last few years getting her teaching degree at night while she worked in an elementary school office during the day. She'd met Tony in a night class, but he wasn't a student; he was her math teacher. Now there would be two teachers in the house. She had a job waiting for her at the same junior college where Tony worked and would be putting her English degree to use next fall.

Rachael turned to her kids, who were lined up at the door of the old green pickup.

"I love you guys," Rachael said, with tears in her eyes. She gathered Kelly and Stevie (who was way too big to be called Stevie since making quarterback for the varsity football team this year, but old habits were hard to break) and pulled them into a group hug.

"Hey, don't leave Dad out of a hug," Tony protested.

The new Battaglia family clung together until Rachael's mother cleared her throat.

"You'd better get going so you don't miss your flight. Don't worry, everything will be just fine. I'll keep an eye on things. Now go have a wonderful honeymoon, you two. I love you."

"We love you too," Tony said. Another hug.

"Hey. Don't forget me!" Ava said, throwing her arms around them.

"We'd never forget you," Tony said.

"Better not, or I may keep Tootie," Ava said.

"Thanks for watching her."

"What are friends for but watching each other's cats?" Ava said and laughed.

Tootie had been Ava's cat to begin with, until they found out Tim was allergic; then the little spoiled cat became Rachael's. Ava planned on introducing Tootie to her new house while Rachael and Tony were on the beaches of Hawaii. Patrick's job, while they were gone, was to move Rachael and the kids' stuff out of her apartment and into their new home. Kathy and the kids were going to clean up the apartment for the next occupants. Mae was going to help not only with fixing up the kids' rooms and getting them settled in, but adding Rachael's stuff to Tony's room. No, no—it was *their* room now.

All Rachael knew was that everything was going to be ready for them when they got back. She didn't have a say in this part, and this was one time when she didn't mind.

"Have a great time, and don't worry about anything!" Kathy yelled.

"Thanks, Kathy. Let us know how the girls are doing," Rachael responded.

"They're almost better. A few more days, I think. The boys had it at their age, and so did your kids. I couldn't bring them here and take the chance of anyone getting it who hadn't had chicken pox. And I couldn't expose the newlyweds before their honeymoon, since you don't know if Tony's had it."

"Yeah, don't worry, sis, we've got this. Just enjoy!" Patrick added.

"Thanks, guys!" Tony waved.

Kathy's attention had shifted to her phone. *Checking on her girls,* Rachael thought.

Rachael looked for her nephews but didn't see them. They were probably playing video games. Rachael couldn't imagine having two three-year-olds, two six-year-olds, plus the boys, too.

Tony grasped Rachael's hand and winked at her. Time to go.

"Goodbye!" Tony and Rachael said together before he helped her into the truck.

"Goodbye, Mom. Goodbye, Dad," Kelly yelled over her brother. They had accepted him as their father, but not Eddie.

Tony pulled away, honking his truck horn, and then slipped in a CD: *Before You.* Settling her head on Tony's shoulder in contentment, Rachael closed her eyes. This was going to be a perfect honeymoon to top off a perfect wedding. There was that word, "perfect"—only now, unlike her first wedding, she knew what it meant, and she dozed off with a smile on her face.

Her dreams should have been peaceful at this point, but they led her back to her first wedding. She saw herself standing in that pale silver dress, so young and hopeful, next to Ed. She'd only known him for six months but thought she had met her Prince Charming. Then her dream took her to opening the package with the snow globe and watching it break. She opened her eyes, but kept her head rested on her new husband's shoulder as they passed the beach she'd always taken her kids to so they could chase the ocean waves.

Thinking of good times didn't rid her of that knot in her stomach. She'd thankfully forgotten about the snow globe during the wedding. She hadn't even told Tony about it yet. Rachael wondered who would send it to her. And why did they write the word "remember" on the bottom? Then there was that face she thought she'd seen in the window when they were dancing.

She was almost positive everyone was watching them dance. How strange—but not as strange as the snow globe. She wasn't going to tell Tony about this until they got back. She didn't want him to worry. Nothing was going to spoil this week for them. She fell back into a fitful sleep as they left Pacifica and headed for the San Francisco airport.

Rachael was woken out of a dreamless slumber with a gentle kiss.

"Naptime's over. Let the honeymoon begin."

"We're here already?" Rachael asked, sitting up and running her fingers through her hair. She pulled it out of the bun and shook it free. She glanced in the truck mirror and smoothed it down so she didn't look like she'd been in a wind tunnel.

"We are, and, might I add, you look amazing," Tony said, helping her out of the pickup into his arms. Her bad thoughts floated away as he began kissing her; gently at first, then more urgently. His hands began to slide down past the small of her back.

"Careful, Mr. Battaglia. You could get us arrested if you begin our honeymoon too soon," Rachael said, pulling away with a smile.

"We have a little time before we need to check in," he said, guiding her back into the pickup. They were rolling around on the truck seat like teenagers when a car pulled into the parking space next to them.

"Now, that's enough! There will be plenty of time for that later," Rachael scolded, sitting up and dabbing lipstick off Tony.

The sour older couple looked at them as though they'd never seen people kissing before. Rachael thought it had to have been a while—like maybe a decade or two—since they'd even held hands. The "Just Married" sign didn't seem to soften them toward Rachael or Tony.

"Maybe we can finish this in the restroom on the plane," Tony said, loud enough for them to hear.

Rachael stifled a laugh and replied in a fake Southern drawl, "It's a long flight, so when the movie starts, so can we. We don't need that cramped bathroom, honey."

The man was as red as his wife as he slammed down his car trunk and hurried away with their luggage. They heard the woman say to him, "I sure hope those two animals aren't on our flight!" The man nodded as they left.

Rachael and Tony burst into laughter, which they ended with one more kiss.

"I bet those two haven't had that much to talk about in a long while. I sure hope we don't get like that," Rachael said, smoothing her hair down again and grabbing a bag as Tony checked the pickup to make sure they weren't forgetting anything.

"We'll never be like that, I promise. Besides, we're starting out with more sparks than those two have probably ever seen in a lifetime. No man with a hot chick like you would ever turn into such an old sourpuss as that."

"Hot chick, really!" Rachael huffed like the older lady and walked off in a snooty fashion, with Tony closing in behind her.

"That's why I love you so much, Mrs. Battaglia," Tony breathed in Rachael's ear.

"I love you too, Mr. Battaglia, but look at the time. We'd better get moving so we don't have to run through the terminal to our plane. Truck locked?"

Tony nodded.

They hurried to the shuttle, through screening, and to the airplane that was waiting to take them to Hawaii. Unfortunately, they never got their date on the plane. Rachael's nerves got the best of her when she sat down in her seat. She took the anti-anxiety pill the doctor had given her. She was skeptical, but it knocked her right out, and she fell asleep in Tony's arms. She didn't wake up until he nudged her.

"Rach, look, there's the island through the clouds."

They'd made it! Rachael hoped her mother's pink luck would get them safely on the ground. It did.

* * *

Ed was watching over Rachael like he was supposed to. He could even see her dreams. How he'd treated her was something he had been reliving since the day he died. He knew the day he married her that she was too good for him. Why hadn't he told her that? Tony seemed to be totally in love with her. Ed understood that, or at least he thought he did. Ed truly wanted Rachael to find happiness, but he had a job to do first. What if Tony wasn't what he seemed? *Could he be part of the problem?* Ed observed the dark entity following along behind Rachael and Tony. It kept its distance from them, but it was never far away.

Ed followed the newly married couple from the airport to their hotel. He pondered over who could have sent that snow globe to her. He knew that figuring that out would help him. Would one of their kids do it? Stevie and Kelly had certainly turned out well, thanks to Rachael. That was apparent at the wedding. That only left Eddie, who wasn't there for his mother. Ed's heart ached when he thought of his oldest son. He had not only failed his wife, but his son. Ed wasn't sure how he was going to make this right.